T0102744

RAGLANDS

The Anamnesis of the Life of "Anwen"

Nikki Goodwin

Order this book online at www.trafford.com
or email orders@trafford.com

Most Trafford titles are also available at major online book retailers.

Printed in the United States of America.

ISBN: 978-1-4669-1461-2 (sc)
ISBN: 978-1-4669-1460-5 (e)

Library of Congress Control Number: 2012903718

Trafford rev. 04/18/2012

www.trafford.com

North America & international
toll-free: 1 888 232 4444 (USA & Canada)
phone: 250 383 6864 • fax: 812 355 4082

CONTENTS

This book is dedicated to Pete and Carol Johnson, who have accepted and supported me without question. You gave me so much of your time to help me find my story, and I thank you.

To Michelle, Ann, and Julianne, who continually encouraged me to write, no matter what the outcome would be or the criticism I might receive.

ACKNOWLEDGMENTS

This book is for my children, Jason and Kerri—my life, my all. Follow your dreams and believe that you can achieve anything you wish. I know now that I will never leave you nor stop loving you.

For Darrell, my husband, who gave me the chance to find Carew, which gave me so much inspiration. You always said I could be more than I thought I could be. There are no words . . .

To my darling mother, who came on my journey. I will carry you in my heart forever.

To my darling Aunty Peg, who encouraged me to take this journey, and whom I love dearly.

PROLOGUE

I was born in Africa in 1966. This soul-searching journey started some six years ago, when I turned forty and took control of my life. I won't bore you with those details, but they're significant, for they opened the doors to a series of amazing events.

From that time, I have had a new thought process, and I now believe the people who come into our lives during our lifetime have significance. I don't believe in random events, and I believe everything is planned. I believe that those people who have wronged us, or whom we have wronged, will continue to do so until we make it right.

As my enlightenment grew, a series of incredible events took place. People from my past started popping up through the medium of social networks, and those who'd wronged me apologised without intervention from me. In this time, so too did those positive people also present themselves, and in February 2009 a very old friend of my parents made contact with me.

During the next couple of months he caught up on news of my family and what we had all been doing for the last twenty-five years. While we were writing to each other, he suggested that I should write a book. Well, like everyone these days, I feel a book seems to be the 'done' thing, and to be honest I was not sure what I *would* write about. A story of 'my life' certainly wouldn't make for interesting reading. So I didn't even entertain the notion. Some weeks passed, till one day I was driving to collect my daughter and the most amazing thing happened to me.

This story just 'popped' into my head. So vivid and so strong was this story that I could 'see' the place, 'smell' the place, and 'feel' the place. It was like I was watching a movie with the physical sensations to go with it. So I rushed home, opened my computer, and started to write it down. I wrote without thought or effort. It was as if someone was writing through me, for when I went back and read what I had written I could not believe what was on the page. Essentially, it's a story of a girl who I believe lived in Wales around the 1500s. She was a peasant girl who had a gift. She worked with herbs and such. She'd had a love affair with the lord of the castle, and it would seem to just be a 'standard fairy-tale story.' The only thing, though, is that I had a sense that this place was more than just a place in a tale. I became excited and invigorated, and since I had not been to Wales and knew no Welsh names, I went online to select names for my characters—names from A-Z.

I envisaged her looking similar to myself, and the name I chose for her was 'Anwen'. Time passed, and during this period of writing I was 'transformed.' I decided that I would make a book of this, and with this in mind, I also wanted to illustrate the cover. So I wrote to my parents' friend in Wales to ask him to please send me some pictures of the hundreds of castles within Wales to give me a reference base to work with. Weeks passed, and of all the castles that come through, none looked anything like the one I could see in my head or know it to be. Until one night he sent through

Carew Castle, in Carew, near Tenby, Wales. I literally fell off my chair, for this was the *exact* place I had pictured in my head.

Herein lies the extraordinary fact. The main part of *my* story (for I have written it as a series of events) is a detailed description of a tournament that I called the 'Day of Festivals' that went on for some five days. It spoke of a banquet in a great hall. On discovering Carew Castle, I then read the history of its existence, and it would appear that it is some two thousand years old and has some kind of paranormal history.

Whether or not you believe in this kind of phenomena, there was an investigation at the castle by a team of 'ghost busters.' The investigator tells of the fact that he can sense a woman of my description dressed in white waiting for her love to return . . . all fairly ambiguous . . . . He then goes on to say that the woman's name is *Anwen*!! He also spoke of two other names that I had selected, very strange Welsh names!!

Now you tell me, of all the names I could have selected, of all the castles I could have chosen, why did this happen? I approached my husband to let me take a trip to Narberth. I had to go there to see it for myself. I took my mother with me as witness to my experience. When I got there, I felt so elated. I have never in my life experienced such joy and peace. I felt as though I had 'come home', so to speak.

I did not hesitate once and walked around the whole castle ruin. I walked straight to the places I had written about. It was like I had lived there my whole life; everything was so familiar to me. I even got in a car and drove around the country roads in the forest surrounding the castle grounds, to the place I believe Anwen lived. At the entrance of the castle, in the courtyard, is a massive herb garden and notices standing testament to the fact that Carew had a history of healing with herbs during the 1500s. Everything I had written, very similarly, seemed to be as it was! I then discovered that the 'Day of Festivals', which I had mentioned in my story, was similar to a historical event marking the knighthood of a Sir Rhys Ap Thomas! An event *he* created. Everything as I had 'felt' it had been mirrored some of what I had written about, for we then took a tour with a guide around the castle and it was very similar to my story. Do you know that in the great hall in *my* story I had accurately stated that there were *two* fireplaces?

I did not 'know' *the entire* castle, only three rooms in the ruin, but I was more familiar with the forests around the castle.

I have now come to understand that there was a reason for this memory. My life has been altered, and since embracing the obvious, the most amazing things continue to happen daily. People are presented to me, and dealing with the challenges of life has been made effortless. I truly believe that I am somehow connected to this lady Anwen, and I believe that the lessons I have to learn are many and the journey of my life will not only continue in this lifetime but will continue until I have learnt all I can learn.

In publishing this tale, everything happened as I have documented it, and as 'fantastical' as it may seem, even to me, I am living it, experiencing it, and can stand testament to it. 'The truth is easy to speak'.

—Nikki Goodwin, 2012

AUTHOR'S NOTE

This story is the Anamnesis (the recalled memory of a life) of the life of a girl named "Anwen" who I believe lived during the 1500's. How this story came to be is the most remarkable experience of my life. I have never written a book before and not for one minute did I have to think about what it was that I was writing. The result of this story has forever changed the path of my life and it has allowed me to find my Soul's purpose, I am currently doing my Doctorate in Metaphysical Hypnosis (Mhyp.D) as a result of this, and plan to reach out and hopefully be able to enlighten others to the wonders of our existence. The Castle exists in Carew, near Tenby, Wales and is called Carew Castle.

The main event of *MY* story, similarly relates to the documented Great Tournament held by Rhys ap Thomas in 1507—one of the most lavish entertainments in the history of Wales. Whilst these events did occur, *MY* story is *NOT* a documented historical occurrence. It is simply a story that seems to be connected to this beautiful place. The names of the characters and everything within MY story are totally fictional. Whilst 'Ragland' castle, does actually exist in Wales; it is very obviously not 'my' castle. I decided to call it 'Raglands', because for me it was a play on words.

What has been written has been etched in time, for what was spoken and thought has manifested physically.

'Take me with you in your heart and feel me holding your hand through this life and into the next,' is what Anwen whispered into my ear as I left the beautiful grounds of the castle.

ABOUT THE AUTHOR

Nikki Goodwin (B.Msc) was born and still lives in Africa. She speaks from the heart, documenting the events of an incredibly brave sixteenth century woman and her will to survive. It highlights the reality that whichever century we have lived in, humanity still seems to face the same challenges. Nikki Goodwin is currently enrolled in a doctorate progam in Metaphysical Hypnosis (Mhyp.D).

CHAPTER ONE

Where it all started . . .

Branwenn looked down at the new baby in her arms, a beautiful baby girl. Now, at long last, she would be able to pass on the secrets that had been passed down to her through the generations. This child was different, and as she looked into her eyes she could see there was a flicker of recognition in them, even though she was just a few hours old. 'Welcome, my darling child', she said. 'I think that your name should be Anwen, for I know that you will be very beautiful. I have seen you in my dreams.'

Branwenn knew Anwen was no normal child. She had a very old soul and hailed from a position of great esteem. She knew also, however, that her new daughter's life would not be easy and that she would have a long and arduous journey ahead of her.

Teleri, who was Branwenn's mother, had been the midwife. She was busy cleaning up the soiled sheets, and as she looked down upon her daughter and new granddaughter, her heart was filled with peace. This beautiful child would bring so much joy to this place, and Teleri recognised, as had Branwenn, that this baby was no ordinary child.

She had been born with a great wisdom. Teleri placed her hand on Branwenn's shoulder and said to her, 'Be still and listen to the noise of the silence. For in that silence you can learn so much.' Branwenn cleared her mind of the immediate noises around her.

Her two sons were very excited about the birth of their new baby sister and were running around the house with much joviality. She took a deep breath, and as she had done so many times before, she became still and listened. She closed her eyes, and as she held her little daughter in her arms this is what she heard: the sound of the wind moving through the trees in the forest, the birds going about their daily task of survival, and the sound of the stream far away over the plain in the untamed forest. Her breathing was calm and even, and here she paused, for she thought she heard a whisper—the whisper of an ancient tongue. Branwenn listened and understood. It said, 'I am Sekhet, and I am reborn.' Branwenn slowly opened her eyes and looked down at her baby. She was smiling up at her.

Glendwyr had never been happier. Born to him this day was a beautiful daughter. Having two healthy sons was already a great blessing, and as a woodcrafter and farmer he valued their help. His eldest son, Aneiron, was very dutiful and always did as he was told while his second son, Cass, would always ask why.

Now his family was complete with a daughter—he knew that she would be great company for his wife, Branwenn. He thought of the many years she had spent helping the people in their village. Branwenn was gifted in the art of healing. His wife was special and different, and because of this the community within their village had not always accepted her. Having a daughter would allow her the opportunity of passing down her knowledge in the arts of healing. Glendwyr remembered the many times he had been witness to the cruelty she had endured as a result of her gift. He knew that his wife longed for a daughter to pass on the knowledge she had received from her mother, Teleri, and the generations that had gone before. And although there had been many times he had wished that his wife was not special, there were many more times that he had been proud. Glendwyr came to understand and respect his wife's talent and never once questioned her reasoning.

The boys were running around making a huge ruckus, so he decided that perhaps it would be a good idea to take them fishing. He left his wife to rest, his beautiful daughter sleeping peacefully at her mother's side.

As he was about to leave, Mary, a neighbour, met him at the front door. She had brought a basket full of treats. Mary was one of Branwenn's closest friends and was the cook at Ragland Castle—the castle that stood majestically over the river, the castle that would be the centre of his daughter's life.

Time passed peacefully, and when Anwen was six years old Branwenn announced that they were going to be parents again. A healthy son was born to them, and they named him Gareth. Anwen had been delighted to have a sibling younger than herself and spent many hours helping her mother tend the baby. Amongst the other duties she tended to, Anwen loved to help her father in the fields. She loved to be around him and her two older brothers.

On one of these particular days, when Anwen was thirteen, she was suddenly filled with urgent need to see her mother. She had been out the whole day in the fields, planting potatoes and tending to the tasks she had been given responsibility for.

Although she had two older brothers she did not want any kind of preferential treatment 'just because she was a girl.' Society had so many rules for girls. Her father wanted her to be taught social graces that would one day win her the hand of a gentleman.

He would have liked her to be wed to a nobleman, but that was out of the question. As a commoner it was more likely she would grow wings than marry a lord.

She was covered in mud, and the dress she wore was stained red from the dirt. It had once been white. She thought to herself, *What a silly colour that was for a dress.* Totally impractical, unless of course you were a lady and did nothing all day except look pretty. Little did she know that *she* was *the* most beautiful girl in the village. At age thirteen she had blossomed into something her parents would never have envisaged.

Anwen picked up the pace to get home before dark. The forest was not nice at night, full of things she was not comfortable with. She was grateful that her mother had taught her which plants to pick for medicinal purposes and which plants were good to eat. She even knew which ones to use to make your food taste nicer. There were those special ones that she had not been shown, which if you dried and burned, created a smoke, that if you inhaled it could even allow you to hear the murmurings of the forest and Mother Nature. People thought her mother was a witch. They were cruel and ignorant.

It always made Anwen angry that those very people who had nothing nice to say about her mother were the very ones who came knocking on her door at all hours of the night or day to obtain something to take the pain out of a bad headache or bellyache . . . some even came to ask for that which could take away the 'indiscretions' of an unwanted pregnancy.

The name Branwenn, as her mother's name, meant 'dark and pure', and Anwen had inherited her mother's jet black, thick, and lustrous hair. Her mother spent an hour a day combing and braiding it. Another thing Anwen believed was a waste of time.

She could see the smoke from the chimney of the small home. It was such a warm-looking home. Very rustic and crude really, but her father had lovingly built this home for her mother, and they thought it was just like Ragland Castle. They all liked to believe it was just as grand. She had heard the stories of how her father—a kind and gentle man who spent his days providing for them all, never once complaining—had chosen the biggest, strongest trees to make this home for his family. Nothing was too much trouble for him and the word no was just not in his vocabulary.

She ran up the three steps to the front door and found it slightly ajar. She could see her mother sitting in front of the fire at her spinning wheel, spinning yarn to make garments that would keep her and her brothers and father warm during the long winter ahead. Anwen paused and thought that her heart was going to break, the pain from the emotion so great that she burst into the room and ran and threw herself sobbing into her mother's arms.

Branwenn was surprised and distressed and pushed her daughter to arm's length to inspect her to make sure that she was not harmed in any way. As she met her daughter's gaze and saw the tears streaming down her cheeks, she knew what was going through the child's mind. They had a bond that was so great that words sometimes just got in the way.

Anwen looked at her mother for a moment and then said, 'I missed you today. I love you so much and don't want you to ever die. Promise me that you will never leave me.'

Branwenn smiled and said, 'My darling, all things die. Our bodies are only given to us as a means to live out that which we are destined to do. But be sure that my soul will live forever and like the souls of everything living I will continue to be for all eternity and I shall always watch over and be at your side for always.'

As she pondered her mother's words, Anwen sat in her mother's arms till the sun had set and they could hear the owl and night creatures waking.

It was a moment she would never forget. She felt so loved, so at peace and one with nature. She felt that she had a purpose and a calling but knew that there would never be anything greater than this moment shared.

CHAPTER TWO

Cedrick

Cedrick was a very insecure little boy. He was a bully. He hadn't always been mean—life just made him that way and he would grow to become a baseless, cruel man. For his insecurities he would find weaker individuals to pick on, for the things he hated most about himself he would pick on others for, making his problems their fault. Fault, that is, in his eyes.

Any time Anwen was around Cedrick, he made her feel insignificant and stupid. She found herself clutching the talisman around her neck as if willing him out of her sight. It was a strange talisman, one that had been passed down to her through her family. She could see that Cedrick so desperately wanted to be loved and accepted by her it became an obsession to control everyone and everything around him.

It frustrated him that he could not control her . . . . The talisman made her feel safe, and as long as she had it she knew he could not touch her. She never took it off and knew he had noticed it. Once he had tried to take it from her and in so doing fell down and split open his lip. She knew why he had been hurt and felt sorry for him but was pleased that she had been spared from his cruelness.

The forest was alive with so many beautiful creatures, so many places that held so many secrets. Anwen spent her childhood exploring the lay of the land and could find her way home in the dark with no hesitation.

Cedrick and his brothers lived on the farm next to theirs. She hated Cedrick. He and his brothers would tease her and follow her around, especially when she went down to the river to fetch water. She could hear them whispering to each other and giggling, hiding behind the trees and bushes. They thought she was oblivious to the fact that they were there. They thought they were like the fabled magician Merlin's apprentices who could make themselves invisible!

They would sneak on to her father's potato farm and pull out the potato seeds she and her brothers and father had planted. She knew they were guilty, and when her father confronted Cedrick's father about it, there was always an altercation. Cedrick lied with a straight face each time, blaming Braith. Braith was Lilybet's and Seren's brother.

Braith was the same age as Cedrick, but of his thirteen years he had the brain function of a five-year-old. He was a simple, gentle soul. Anwen swore that one day she would punch Cedrick in the stomach just for all the nasty things he did to Braith.

After Anwen had finished taking food to her father and brothers in the field, she was asked to please deliver a pie to Cedrick's mother. Anwen hated going to their farm; it meant that she would be faced with all the boys standing behind their mother pulling rude faces at her and making lewd gestures.

When she got to the front door she could hear the boys shouting at the top of their voices. Una, Cedrick's mother, was cursing and yelling, complaining that she could not take much more of their behaviour. She was busy telling them that it was bad enough that she had to put up with their father, who would give her a beating every night just because she had not done something a certain way.

Anwen had heard it spoken between her parents that Owain was a cruel and vile man, and it was no wonder his sons had turned out the same way. Una was crying and clearly very agitated, for it would appear that Cedrick and his brothers had not delivered their father's lunch.

The boys had decided today that they would rather go fishing, and whilst they were down by the river they took it upon themselves to eat the meal prepared especially for their father.

Anwen hesitated and then knocked very loudly to be heard above the din. Una came to the door red-faced and puffy-eyed. Her right eye was a shade of blue and yellow from a beating she had obviously recently endured. She smiled when she saw Anwen. She loved this beautiful child and it made her sad that she had not been blessed with a daughter like her. She certainly could have done with the help within the household.

After greeting her politely, Anwen announced that her mother had sent over a meat pie for them. She explained that her brothers had been called to accompany Lord Blathaon's son, Winn, on a hunt. What Lord Blathaon didn't realise was that her brothers were very experienced hunters and their takings for the day would have given them one of the wild boars they had killed. Una jumped forward and threw her arms around Anwen, showering her with kisses. This would save her from another beating. Anwen pulled away and politely dried her face of the spit and tears.

Una then asked Anwen if she would take this pie to Owain at the church, where he worked, for his dinner. When Cedrick stepped forward to take the task, his mother turned and hit him very hard on the right side of his ear, telling him he would not even get to smell this pie and that the next time he would step foot out of the house would be in the morning when he would have to go and empty the chamber pots as his punishment.

Anwen felted panicked with the request, but as her parents had taught her she obediently accepted the errand. After all, she was not stupid. She knew she was going to save this poor woman from another beating.

Anwen left their house a little apprehensive. The church was quite a distance from home, farther even than the castle. She would not have time to turn back to tell her mother what Una had asked her to do. She hoped her mother would realise where she had been sent. Her mother always knew everything about everything. Anwen could never understand how.

However, Anwen loved going to the church. It was such a beautiful building, and the cemetery around the church was tended to by the holy man. Anwen was fascinated by the church. Her family was not welcome there (the town folk thought they dabbled in witchcraft, which of course was ridiculous!) but on many an occasion Anwen had sneaked away from her daily chores in the field on a Sunday. She would slip in quietly and hide behind the open door. From there she had a clear view of the whole church. She would watch how the children pretended to be listening. Some would be sleeping, and others, like Cedrick, would be causing a commotion.

Owain helped in the gardens of the church and because of this he felt that he was considered a religious man. The fact that he beat his wife and drank himself senseless whenever he had the chance was beside the point. He knew nothing of being a spiritual person. He knew nothing of the laws of nature and had no respect for the beauty around him.

Anwen loved to walk around the cemetery reading the headstones. She could imagine the people lying beneath her and could never understand how it was that only the noblemen and people of stature were able to be buried here. The loved ones who passed from her village were buried atop the mountain and within the 'untamed forest.' The place that her father had picked for their final resting place was quite a climb up a mountain. The view from the top though would make the journey all that more worth the while. Only her grandfather was buried there, and from time to time she would make the journey with Teleri to tend to his grave.

He certainly did not have a fancy headstone like those within the church graveyard. His was made from wood, carved by her father. A beautiful birch tree had given itself to mark his passing. It read 'Here lies Glyndwyr 1350-1416. Beloved of his family, returned to whence he came' and the symbol of the amulet her grandmother had passed down to her mother was carved into the wood. Anwen knew that one day it would be hers to wear.

Whilst walking through the untamed forest Anwen was particularly aware of the fact that she was being watched. The creatures within the forest were many. Many, though, could only be seen by a select few. Teleri and her mother, Brannwenn, had told her of the delicate forest creatures, those of myth and fairy tale. And this was how they were remembered by those of the village, stories that were told to the children to keep them obedient. Anwen smiled. Even in her young years she was far wiser than most and felt sorry for those who could not 'see.' She knew one day it would be her turn.

As she climbed the hill to the church a little way ahead she noticed Seren carrying a basket with flowers in it. Seren was older than Anwen, in her early twenties, Anwen imagined. She had fair hair and brown eyes. Seren, like Braith, was also 'simple.' When she had been in her mother's womb, the poor pregnant woman had fallen into the river and almost drowned. Now, although Seren was definitely a woman on the outside, she was definitely a child in every other way, as simple as a child of ten.

Anwen picked up the pace to catch up with her. Perhaps she could help her arrange the flowers for the church service this Sunday. She saw Owain working in the graveyard clearing weeds. He moved towards the church door, hesitated, and looked back before entering. Anwen assumed he too was going to speak to Seren. She felt relieved that she was not going to be alone with this awful man. It would take all of her willpower to remain polite. Now at least she would not have to make conversation. She could simply hand over the pie and make her way back home. This would now give her time to pass 'the Tree' and maybe even catch a glimpse of those very special creatures.

As Anwen approached the door of the church she heard Seren whimpering like an animal, above which she could hear Owain. Anwen could not understand what it was that he was asking Seren to do, but she could tell that it was something Seren was very uncomfortable with.

As Anwen poked her head around the door she saw Owain force Seren up against the pulpit. With his back to her and his body size being double that of Seren's, it was difficult to see exactly what it was that he was doing. All

Anwen could see were Seren's arms flailing about, pulling and pushing as hard as she could.

A huge knot formed in the pit of her stomach as she realised that if she did not speak up, something even worse was about to happen. At the top of her voice she called out, 'Father Tad.' Her voice was barely audible, and she ran forward, shouting, 'Father Tad, Father Tad! Is it okay if I help Seren with the flowers?'

Owain spun around, almost throwing Seren away from him. She lost her balance, and she and the pulpit went flying.

Owain stood there with his pockmarked red face, bulbous nose, and tiny little piggy eyes glaring at Anwen. A very fat man who (if they existed) Anwen thought would look just like a troll.

The blood drained from her face, and she thought that her heart would burst from her chest.

Seren was busy gathering herself off the floor, picking up the pulpit, and trying to salvage the blooms that had been scattered everywhere. Sweating and covered in dirt, he moved towards her. Anwen thrust the pie forward into his face, which brought him to a halt. Seren stood watching, too afraid to even breathe.

Anwen took a deep breath and proceeded to tell him that his wife had made this pie especially for his lunch and that she had met Cedrick and his brothers on their way to bring him his meal.

Owain was about to let rip, when from the side of the church, came, 'Well now, isn't that a treat for you, Owain. Can we trade lunches?' Owain took the pie and marched out of the church, mumbling something about how Anwen was always interfering with things.

Father Tad told Anwen that he had heard her request and had come hastily, due to the commotion that was ensuing within his church. Anwen knew that Father Tad knew what had happened. Thankfully she did not have to say anything. Besides, she was quite sure he would talk to Seren about it. Seren smiled and hugged Anwen so hard she could hardly breathe. She thanked her, and with a look of a secret shared, she handed her the basket. The two of them continued to decorate the church, and after which they left hand in hand, with Father Tad watching till they were out of sight within the 'untamed forest.'

CHAPTER THREE

Aneirin, Cass, and Gareth

The trees in the forest were like friends to Anwen, and each one had a meaning. Each was like a friend to her, and they kept her safe and made her feel like she was part of something bigger and more important than herself.

On this particular day she was going fishing with her three brothers. Anwen loved spending time with them. Each had his own unique character, and although you could tell they were all related, each of the children had his or her own unique 'look.' Her oldest brother was tall and had very dark curly hair. His eyes were a very light brown; his complexion was darker than hers. Aneirin was the 'gentle giant' of the family and was similar to her father in nature.

He could never say no, especially to his little sister, and Anwen knew that she had him 'hook, line, and sinker.' Aneirin would always take the time to show her things that only men were supposed to know, such as how to hold an axe to chop wood. He explained that if you held it too far near the end of the shaft you could not wield enough power to allow the axe to go through the wood cleanly. The axe would get stuck in the wood. And as she soon learnt, this was the most annoying thing to happen if you had a job to get through, spending your time with your foot on the other end of the axe trying to manoeuvre it out of the blasted piece of tree! He showed her how important it was to make sure that you planted your crops in straight lines, leaving enough room to be able to work the field without destroying the crop. He also taught her how to thread a fishing pole. Yes, her oldest brother was the most patient person she knew, save for her father. Anwen loved Aneirin with all her heart.

Cass was so different from the rest of them. His hair was almost white and very curly; his eyes were blue. Cass was the thinker of the family. He was always asking questions and always questioning the answers. It would drive Anwen mad! Although she too had a very inquisitive mind, she was not interested in the *how* it happened, just that it did. Cass lived in his own little world and was very sensitive to people and their feelings. He would sit quietly on the outside of a conversation and assess and analyse each thing that was said.

Gareth was the mischievous brother. He was always getting into trouble for doing something he was not meant to. Anwen spent her life trying to get him out of trouble. He loved to spar and fight and imagined that one day he would be a knight. He was a dear, dear boy and looked at life like it was one big game.

However, when the three boys were together it was a glorious combination. Anwen could sit for hours just listening and watching her brothers interact, watching them rolling around with each other, jousting, and play wrestling. The camaraderie between them touched her heart, and she knew they were unique and special.

She also realised they were the result of having two such wonderful parents. They were decent, grounded, hardworking people who felt it their duty to make sure their children went into the world decent, grounded, and hardworking. They were caring individuals who would never benefit by causing another human being a disservice.

One of the many wonderful days of her early adolescence was when she went fishing with her three brothers. It was a glorious day. She could hear the seagulls closer to Ragland Castle. The forest was buzzing with the noise of the life within and the air was so sweet it hit the back of her throat, and she could taste it in her mouth. After finishing her chores she ran out the house to join them, and they walked hand in hand down to the special point in the river where the fishing was best.

Aneirin knew exactly where to take them. He never came home without enough fish to feed the family a hearty dinner.

Anwen laid out a blanket on the banks of the river. Each of her brothers were fixing up their fishing lines. The game was on. Who would catch the biggest fish today? Each wanted to outdo the other, for to gain Anwen's favour was the biggest reward.

The brothers loved their sister more than life itself. They knew that she was special, and everywhere she went she brought happiness. To gain her favour meant they would have the chance to sit and brush her hair.

Anwen hated having her hair brushed. It took so long, so to have one of her brothers do it was a great relief. They always fought over the brush. It made her smile, if only they knew!

She watched as Aneirin's line hit the surface of the water. The rippling circles reached outward in perfect symmetry.

It always amazed her how precise nature was in its beauty and form. That everything was perfectly measured. The line glistened in the sun, and Aneirin looked across and winked at her.

Cass was busy trying to work out which way the wind was blowing and how fast the current of the stream was running. He was convinced that this would give him the perfect place to tap into a school of fish. Once he had his line in the water he shouted over to Aneirin that he was standing on the wrong side of the river and that the wind would bring his line too far down the stream and get it caught in the reeds. Aneirin just smiled.

Gareth was knee deep in the water. He figured that if he couldn't catch the fish with his line, he would simply reach in and grab one. He was splashing around, and Anwen could not resist the impulse to join him in the water. She winked at Aneirin and Cass and ran straight for her younger brother. She landed on him, throwing him face forward into the water. He turned and pulled her under the water. The two of them were rolling around, splashing and laughing. He loved his bigger sister; she was so spontaneous and fun loving.

Cass was glaring at her and was put out that she was disturbing the water and his chance to catch the first fish. Anwen felt chastised and kissed Gareth on the cheek and left him to gather himself and find his line to put into the water again.

She took off and sat inside the big tree, the special tree where she and her brothers would hide and play in. It was cool, and the smell of the moss and Cipbar bush made her feel welcome.

She stripped down to her underclothes and hung her dress over a branch to dry. She then plaited her hair and went to make a fire to warm herself. Once she had done this she saw that Aneirin had caught the first fish of the day. It was a large one too. Its skin was an iridescent silver-green colour that glistened in the sun. Aneirin told her that it was a male fish and that was the reason it was so handsome, for this fish would have to attract a mate.

Anwen felt saddened that now this fish would not get to do this. So she said a prayer of thanks to Mother Nature for the gift of this food. She took it and sat down to prepare the fish as her brothers had shown her. As she was cleaning the fish something fell out of its stomach. It was the most beautiful stone she had ever seen. She knew that this was something special. This stone belonged to the person who had found it. It was an incredible deep blue with flecks of silver. She picked it out and washed it off in the river. She walked over to her older brother and handed it to him. Anwen told him what Teleri had explained to her, that indeed this stone was his. He had found his colour in this world. She told him to keep it safe and not to show it to anyone who might want to possess it.

Aneirin didn't understand his little sister, yet he had seen enough in his lifetime that he could not explain. So he took it and put it in his pocket, kissing her on her forehead.

Cass and Gareth looked on and both said a prayer to Mother Nature to give them the gift of their stones.

CHAPTER FOUR

The Day of Festivals and Winn

Time had passed, and now, at eighteen, Anwen woke filled with excitement, for today was the 'Day of Festivals.' She knew that she would get to see 'him.' Every twenty years a commoner was selected to oversee the tournament and wear the 'Warrior of the Day' sash. She had heard it whispered in the forest that fate would smile on her and grant her this wish.

After her beloved family had died, Anwen found it hard to look around and pay heed to the teachings her mother had imparted on her. She found it hard to believe that she could be 'connected' to that charred mass of bodies that had once been her family. There was certainly no beauty in it, and she had not yet found the lesson from it.

She moved to the doorway of her new lodging. Teleri had taken her in and promised she would continue to teach Anwen those things her mother had showed her. Teleri was Anwen's grandmother and her only surviving family member, outcast by society for being a 'witch' but having been clever enough to avoid the fate her mother and father and brothers had fallen victim to—the ignorance of people who didn't understand that life was more than the things we could see.

As she looked through the doorway she could see the sunlight hit the mist, dissolving its icy hold on the earth. She could smell the ashes in the hearth and for the first time in months felt happy to be alive. Well, actually, if truth be told this was the second time she had felt happy to be alive. Yesterday was the first! Teleri had asked Anwen to go down to the stream to collect water—the stream where all of her life-changing moments seemed to have occurred. It was the sacred meeting place of the worlds she lived in and the place where she felt safe to learn and to rest.

Yesterday as she came 'round the corner, however, she stopped dead in her tracks, for in the water was a man. He was naked to the waist and stood knee deep. He was running his hands through his thick curly hair, and she remembered that she had been awestruck by his appearance.

Now, Anwen had brothers, and seeing a naked man certainly was not something new. Her brothers had been fair of face and strongly built and it had been said that they were, in fact, as she was, the most beautiful in the village. Anwen used to tease them about being called 'beautiful.' But this creature standing before her was indeed that—a creature—for no human being could possibly invoke such fierce fascination.

She stepped forward to get a closer look, and as she did she stepped on a twig. The noise startled him, and he turned and met her gaze. His eyes were ice blue, and as he held her stare she felt an explosion of warmth between her legs. This response so startled her that Anwen turned and ran.

CHAPTER FIVE

Teleri asked Anwen to please sweep the hearth. She sighed, but not because of the request but because she was in love. Or something like it, for she had never been in love before, and the excitement she felt was almost too much to bear. She planned on being very busy this morning till midday when the tournament and selection would start. She knew that after her tasks for the day Teleri would help her do her hair in a manner that would befit the occasion.

Anwen dressed herself carefully, making sure that all the ties on her bodice were exact. She knew that the dress she was wearing was old and worn, but it was clean and neat. Teleri had spent most of an hour brushing Anwen's long black hair and braiding it with white flowers to match the colour of her dress, for white was the only colour that could be worn on the Day of Festivals. She made sure she'd washed her hair in the ointment her grandmother made. It was a secret ointment, the smell of which was so subtle but so intoxicating. Teleri told her that it had been passed down through the ages and that one day she would tell Anwen how to make it.

Anwen ran down to the stream, careful not to step in any mud, and checked her appearance before she made her way to the castle grounds. As she looked at her reflection in the water she felt sure that 'he' would like what he saw. Even though she knew she was wrong, she hoped that surely love had no class distinction and he would immediately take her for his wife.

The castle grounds were teeming with people she knew well, and she struggled to get to the front of the crowd. Lord Blathaon would have to select the recipient of this great honour. Commoner's being allowed to interact with Lords and Ladies. Each person wishing to partake had brought a personal belonging. They were to place it in a sack, and if he picked it out that person would be the lucky candidate.

Anwen handed forward a handkerchief her mother had embroidered. It was made from the same fabric her dress had been stitched in.

She felt 'his' eyes on her as she placed the handkerchief in the sack. She could read the thoughts of his mind that he secretly hoped she would win, and she felt her face flush. It was a great honour to be selected, for not only did you get to sit on the podium and watch over the ceremonies, afterward you were allowed to participate in the festivities within the castle walls. If selected Anwen would be seated next to the winner of the tournament, whoever he may be. She felt slightly anxious, for there were three possibilities and only one could be a choice.

Next he called for the tassels of the men competing. It was a totally random selection and was left to fate as to whose keepsake would be selected to pair with whose tassel. She smiled because she knew in the pit of her stomach whose tassel she would hold. The forest had told her.

As Lord Blathaon called out the first contestant she watched out of the corner of her eye as Cedrick glared at her. He was making rude gestures towards her, trying to catch her attention to tell her that in his mind, since she was a commoner like he was, she would have his tassel and he would have her to himself. She thought she could feel her skin peel off her body at the thought, like a snake shedding its skin.

There were only five participants in the jousting tournament, and when Cedrick and 'he' were the last two selected, she felt a little panicked. However, Cedrick's face dropped when Lord Blathaon pulled out the hair tie belonging to a very round red-haired girl from the village.

Anwen was the last to be chosen, so it was obvious whose tassel she would hold. 'He' had been distracted preparing his horse and jousting stick for the ceremony, clearly not particularly worried about this part of the ceremony. He just wanted to get on with the actual event. So he did not notice who was to hold his tassel.

Anwen tried three times to catch his attention. She was seated on the podium watching the jousting—he was so beautiful, his jet black hair glistening in the sun. She could only just see the form of his body beneath his armour, but she knew what he looked like because just the day before she had seen him down by the stream—that fateful day when the earth had seemed to stand still. That day he turned, startled by the noise, when he saw her standing there and met her gaze with his piercing blue eyes. She knew then that her life as she knew it would never be the same. Not now, not ever.

Her heart was racing now thinking of their encounter. She tried hard to pay attention to the contest at hand but beads of sweat formed on her upper lip, her breath raspy and uneven. She could feel her nipples harden. Oh, God! Why wouldn't he just look at her! Surely he knew she was watching him, locking him in a gaze that would burn a hole through most things!

The wind blew and she caught his scent. He smelt like rain as it hit the earth, but not . . . like cinnamon, but not. He smelled like no other man on earth and all she knew was that she had to have him. The moment seemed to hang in the air, suspended in time.

As she sat there her life moved in and out of her memory, forming shadows in the corners of her recognition. She did not understand why she was so drawn to this dark knight, why she felt like she knew every inch of his being. Her heart ached and she felt like her skin was on fire . . . and what name did this handsome lord go by? His name was Winn, and he had been so-named since he was so handsome that the breath was literally sucked from your lungs just by glancing at him.

Anwen knew she was certainly not worthy. A man such as Winn was promised to a lady of royalty. How could life be so cruel? Yet he had seen her that day down by the stream, and she knew that the moment they had shared was ancient. It reeked of love, of wanting, of a pureness true and righteous.

Bronwen the redheaded girl shook her shoulders to catch Anwen's attention to tell her the tournament between their chosen men was about to begin.

The jousting tournament was so exciting to watch; definitely one of the highlights of the day. Each knight had his favourite steed, and Winn's horse was the most magnificent animal, a huge white stallion. His mane was a beautiful silver grey and his eyes were a very light brown. His shoulder was as tall as a man, and to mount him Winn needed assistance.

Anwen thought about how forbidding they looked together as a team and was sure that any opponent would feel intimidated before they even started.

Cedrick had already won two of his melees and it was now his turn to fight Winn in the final for the prize of the day—to sit at the head table in Ragland Castle.

The crowd that had gathered hushed, and Winn and Cedrick took their positions, jousting lances in hand, armour fixed in place, helmets secured. This was not a sport for weaklings, and Anwen had heard many tales of those unfortunates who had lost their arms, legs, and sometimes even their heads when they were thrown off their horses.

Lord Blathaon gave the signal, and as his hand dropped the two steeds charged towards each other. Winn leaned forward a little to put his weight into the charge, the horses' hooves tearing at the ground as they raced forward. As they met in the middle both missed and their jousting lances met air. The crowd let out a unified sigh. The horses and their riders turned to ready themselves for the next charge.

This time Winn looked up at the podium and finally noticed Anwen. She thought she noted that he hesitated and was taken aback. It was as though he suddenly realised who was holding his tassel and what it would mean for him to lose this fight.

He turned to face his opponent with a new resolve, and as his steed charged forward he moved sideways in his saddle, giving him a different angle. This put Cedrick in an awkward position, and he could not adjust himself in time to miss the oncoming rider. Winn connected and knocked Cedrick clean out of his saddle. His foot got caught in the stirrup and he was pulled through the brush for a short distance. The horse came to a standstill when it realised it no longer had a rider, and the crowd strained to see if

Cedrick was done for. Being a stocky man though, he was not badly injured. He sat up and shook his head, pulling his helmet off.

Slowly he got to his feet and stumbled towards the podium, where he witnessed Winn receiving the tassel from Anwen. Although he had not been physically injured, Cedrick felt like his heart had been torn from his chest. He had so wanted to win this fight. It was so important to him to show Anwen that he was a worthy suitor and to make her finally see him in a favourable way.

Cedrick had loved her for so many years, and it was becoming harder and harder for him to control his desires and anger. Bronwen came running across the field, her soft rotund body hurtling towards him, her extremely large breasts bouncing all over the place. He felt repulsed by her and in comparison to Anwen she was extremely ugly. He would have to endure her affections for the night, and he thought that perhaps after the meal and much mead in his belly she would look less like a pregnant swine, and, in fact, he may even relieve his tensions on her.

Winn took the tassel from Anwen, his heart beating so loudly he thought she could hear it through his armour. The excitement he felt knowing that he would be seated next to this beautiful woman for the night was almost too much to imagine. He had to get through the rest of the day though, and there were still many tournaments to be fought, including the stone throwing, the tug-of-war, and the archery. He didn't want to participate in any of them now; all he wanted was to take his prize and steal her away from the crowds.

CHAPTER SIX

The day passed and he watched from a distance as Anwen took part in the ladies' tug-of-war (those from the village only). She was second from the front and had tucked her dress up so as not to get it dirty. He watched as she shouted and encouraged the ladies on her side not to give up. She was red in the face, and with her determination to stay clean he knew that there was no way she was going to land in the mud. Poor old Bronwen was on the end of the opposing side, and when Anwen's team pulled them over she landed in the mud waist deep. Cedrick smirked and thought how fitting it was. His swine in the mud!

Anwen dropped the rope and quickly adjusted her dress so that she 'looked' like a lady again—smoothing it down over her hips, rubbing her palms clean of the sweat. Her hands were red and felt scathed. It hadn't been easy pulling over that lot!

Winn watched her as she took the young girls of the village over to the flower threading table. This was where the girls around six years of age would take the flowers picked from the fields and the ivy and thread them together to create a table decoration for the head table for the banqueting dinner.

All the girls were dressed in white, and it was so natural and innocent watching them laughing and singing as they worked. There were the musicians from the castle and all the entertainers, the villagers, who included the blacksmith and his wife and family, the villagers who grew food for the village, the village physician, and the castle physician. The court jesters and the cooks and maids were all singing and dancing. It was a day to remember.

The festival had run for five days, and as the sun began to set the crowd knew they had to gather at the entrance to the castle, where as part of the closing ceremony they would witness the setting of the sun. Here they would light huge bonfires and do a ceremonial dance, singing a chant to encourage a good harvest, favourable weather, and health to the village. It was important that everyone took part in this ritual, and even those who could not walk were required to in some way move around the fire and recite the ancient reading. It was taught to every child from the time they were able to speak, and since this tournament only happened once every twenty years, not many people attended more than once in their lifetime. Teleri had been to three and she was one of the few who had.

Anwen stood at the front of the crowd with the fire blazing hot on her face, since she was part of the favoured group this twilight. As she began to move around the fire she felt herself slipping away from the crowd. She was hypnotised by the dancing flames, intoxicated on the happiness of the day, and she allowed herself to drift off. She could barely hear herself reciting the chant that she knew so well. She could recite it in her sleep. She could barely hear the crowd and even forgot her beautiful Winn opposite her on the other side of the fire.

Anwen closed her eyes and opened her mind as her mother had taught her, and she was taken to a land that was so different from this one. It was not green and lush but dry and sandy. She saw strange castles in the sand. They were also made from stone but had a thick base, and they thinned as they reached up, pointing into the sky. They were beautiful and majestic—so different from the castles of home.

She felt herself floating through the corridors of one of these massive buildings, and it was cool and the air was scented. The scent was familiar to her, similar to the one Teleri had washed her hair in. There was much richness and grandeur, gold trimmings and white linen. Anwen was drawn to a gold basin in one of the larger rooms, and as she looked into the water she saw through her eyes not her own reflection but that of another woman. And yet she knew it to be herself. The woman she was looking at had olive skin and her eyes were darker than her own, almost black. As she looked at the reflection she could see herself in the face of this woman that stared back at her, she instinctively knew that it was herself.

This woman was naked to the waist, and around her waist hung a gold cord. On her head she wore a gold headdress. Anwen reached forward to touch the reflection in the water, and as she did she felt a hot sensation on her hand and could smell burning flesh. She was startled back to reality to notice that it was her hand she could smell burning and she realised that she was holding her hand towards the burning flames of the bonfire.

Tears welled in her eyes and she brought her hand to her mouth to suck it. Winn moved around from the other side of the bonfire to see if there was something he could do, but before he could get to her Teleri appeared. He watched as she pulled a jar of ointment from under her aprons and rubbed it on the blister that was forming. Anwen wiped away the tears from her eyes and stood for a moment trying to understand what it was that she had just witnessed.

She tried to tell Teleri what had just happened but her grandmother looked at her with a look of knowing and said, 'Later child, later.'

Anwen quickly joined back into the chant and as it came to its completion there was an eerie moment as the sun slipped away and the blanket of darkness moved over towards them. Everyone watched as sparks from the bonfire filtered up into the night sky like fireflies on a pilgrimage. The crowd stood still and a deathly hush prevailed. Lord Blathaon stepped forward, and in his booming voice said, 'Let the feast begin!'

Winn moved over to take Anwen on his arm, and as they walked through the gates of the castle it felt like this was the day that Anwen had been waiting for. They walked through the gates and through the courtyard entrance into the main hall. There the room was lit with burning torches placed on the walls at intervals. Two huge fireplaces were at each end of the hall, the heat from which warmed the room and made it cosy and inviting. To the right of the room was a stairwell that led up to the first floor of the castle where, as she was later told, were the sleeping rooms of Lord Blathaon and his wives and Winn and his brothers and sisters. Lord Blathaon was the lord of the castle and Winn's father.

The banister along the stairwell was beautifully carved, a dragon's head formed the base of the railing, its body and tail running up the length of the rail. The wood was familiar and so was the design. She realised then that this was the work of her father. She remembered he had been asked by the lord to create this banister from the trees he had selected to build part of the home he had made for their family. Since he was not entitled to cut the trees down for his own use a special dispensation had been granted him if he made these banisters for the castle.

Anwen's father could have taken stock or food in payment but chose the trees. She felt a huge sadness as she thought of those beautiful old trees that had been cut down, crafted with love to build the home that she and her family had lived in, and were now nothing but ashes blowing on the winds of the plains of Wales.

CHAPTER SEVEN

The Banquet

The room was filling with the crowd. Winn led Anwen to the main table and the two were seated in the middle. Lord Blathaon was seated to the right of Anwen, and his wife was seated to the left of Winn. Winn loved his mother; she was a striking woman and had a kind and gentle nature.

Cedrick, as runner-up, and his lady were then seated appropriately at the head table next to Lord Blathaon. On the outer side of Winn's mother was the second runner-up and his lady. The head table then seated eight people. The girls from the village had done justice to the decorations, and if Anwen didn't know any better this could easily have been a wedding celebration. The only thing spoiling the head table was that there was no way she would have had Cedrick seated there! In fact, he would not even have been present at the ceremony.

The castle musicians were making merriment on their instruments and the music bounced off the stone walls of the castle. Some of the notes seemed to be lost, and Anwen imagined that the castle itself had absorbed the melody to be captured in the cataclysm of the masonry held for all eternity in its memory of the ages. Winn touched her arm and asked her if she was okay. At last she could finally take the time to devote herself to this man who had consumed her thoughts for the last six days.

As he spoke to her, she could not believe how his voice sounded. It was as familiar as the back of her hand and made her feel safe and loved. After accepting a goblet of mead, Lord Blathaon stood up and banged hard on the table with his fist. The room slowly came to a quiet, and he introduced the people at the head table. Anwen felt so insignificant as he said, 'Anwen, daughter of Glendwyr, woodcrafter and potato farmer.' But she felt better when he said, 'Cedrick, son of Owain, potato farmer.' At least her father had had two crafts! She shivered as she thought of Owain and his sons.

Cedrick puffed up at his introduction and she thought he felt as if he was very important.

The evening's festivities were to begin with a ceremonial dance. It was a dance that only lords and ladies were sure to know. She saw panic on Winn's face, and her heart swelled with love when she understood that he wanted to save her from the embarrassment of not being able to appropriately participate. However, Teleri had taught Anwen the art of fancy dancing, and when she indicated to Winn that they very definitely could participate; she saw how surprised he was. As he reached out and took her hand she felt like she had come full circle. Her head was swimming in the pools of memories past. She felt like she had done this before. He looked at her with the same recognition, but he did not hold the same thought for long, and as his eyes lost the moment, he wiped his hand on his chest and lifted her from her seat.

As they walked to the dance floor to take their places next to Lord and Lady Blathaon, Cedrick, Bronwen and the others, she felt the eyes of the audience on them. Winn stood in front of her, and as she made eye contact with him nothing else seemed to matter. All she could think of was how he smelled as he stepped forward and moved in and out of her personal space. She was reminded again that he smelled of rain as it hit the earth, of cinnamon but not . . . oh, this beautiful man.

CHAPTER EIGHT

Cedrick

The evening was a happy time for almost everyone who participated. Even those with physical afflictions were able to participate and enjoy some kind of merriment. Cedrick, however, as hard as he tried, could not accept that he was there with Bronwen, not Anwen. He watched her every move and noticed how she looked at Winn and how he was totally taken with this beautiful woman he had known most of his life. A rage built inside him, and as he drank more and more he found it hard to contain himself.

After the meal he went outside to relieve himself behind a tree at the bonfire. Unfortunately, at that moment, Bronwen had just walked out of the area that had been designated for the women to go and tend to their womanly functions. He overheard her telling one of the other ladies that Anwen was so lucky to have the affections of Winn and that in her opinion this would be the start of a long love affair. They were giggling like stupid little girls. She was giggling and snorting and wheezing and she sounded just like the pig he believed her to be. Pigs were only good for one thing. They ate the rubbish you threw out, and the waste they produced made your potatoes grow stronger. Besides, pigs made a wonderful meal. Bronwen was a pig after all and was expendable. She deserved to be treated like one.

Cedrick waited for the other girl to move out of earshot and then he called out to her. Bronwen was so excited that Cedrick had stopped her. She thought he was so strong and so handsome. She had his tassel, and he was her 'Winn.' She eagerly ran over to him.

Cedrick thought not only was she ugly, she was also dim-witted, and it was going to be very easy to do what he needed to do. He had to do it, for if he didn't he wouldn't be able to go back into the hall and participate like he was expected to. He had come in second that day after all.

Cedrick put his arm around her and took her into the forest. He told her that she was so beautiful and that he was so jealous of all the people in the hall. He wanted to have her to himself for just a second. She blushed and gladly went with him. The rage within him moved through him, and he had only just gotten her out of sight when he felt himself turn. He hit her across the head and knocked her down. Bronwen was completely taken off guard and the wind was knocked from her lungs as she hit the ground. Before she knew what was happening Cedrick flung himself on top of her and tore the dress from her breast. He pulled at her to free her huge bosom from the bodice of her garment. His mouth was over hers, and she could not scream or breathe or call out. When he had her breast in his hand he moved his mouth to her nipple and bit it off.

The air was sucked from her lungs with the pain and she did not know what she had done to deserve this. Cedrick tasted her blood in his mouth, and it excited him. He lifted her skirts and undid the tie to his trousers. His manhood was as hard as a rock and all he could think about was that she was a pig and he was going to give her what pigs deserved. He turned her over onto her stomach, for she was too ugly to look at, and he relieved himself. She stopped moving after a while, and when he had finished he realised that she had stopped moving because he had her around her throat and that in fact she had stopped breathing. He lay on top of her, for he was breathing heavily and his legs felt like jelly.

He felt so much better now and knew now he would be able to go into the hall and perform in the manner in which he was expected. As he lay there he heard his father calling him. He stood up, tied his trousers, and straightened his shirt. He took some leaves off a tree and wiped his face clean. Quickly he pulled Bronwen's body into a tree that had fallen and decayed. The wolves would eat her. Or perhaps he would let his pigs out and they could finish her off. He thought, *Do pigs eat other pigs? That would be interesting to see.*

He went back to the hall, the life he had taken as inconsequential as the dying flower decorations on the table in the hall.

The tradition was that the festivities had to be completed by midnight. Folklore told of those folk who had not made sure that they were tucked away in their beds before midnight. Their crops had failed and their babies had been born deformed. There was only two ways that they could put things right. One was to seek the help of Anwen's mother or grandmother (no one wanted to be seen to be asking them) or to wait it out till the next Day of Festivals and since this took place only every twenty years, no one dared evoke the wrath of something they did not understand. So no sooner had Cedrick rejoined the party when Lord Blathaon called to the castle musicians to cease the music.

The crowd sighed and began to gather themselves and their belongings. The children from the village had been housed in one of the rooms upstairs. They had had a wonderful evening sneaking out from time to time to see their parents dancing and enjoying themselves. The adults knew how lucky they had been to be part of this day and knew that never again, possibly in their lifetime, would they get the chance to be inside this beautiful castle.

Braith's youngest sister, Lilybet, had been paying particular attention to Anwen and Winn. She looked so beautiful that day. She was a particularly perceptive child and had spent many hours with Anwen and her grandmother. Anwen had been so kind to her brother. Her darling brother had been the laughing stock of the village. Anwen had always stood by him and protected and loved him. Braith had loved her so till that day down at the river. That day when it was said that Braith had 'slipped' whilst fishing and fallen in and drowned. She knew better. She knew that one day she would be able to speak out. At thirteen she was not allowed to speak her mind. She knew what had happened. She had overheard Anwen speaking to her grandmother. She had also been privy to the goings on from within Cedrick's household . . . . She hated him so she had watched him like a hawk and had noted the look on Cedrick's face when he had fallen off his horse and watched as Anwen gave Winn his tassel.

She had also seen him leave the room after the meal and had noted that Bronwen had left just before. She was disturbed to note that Bronwen was not at the closing of the ceremony and wondered where she could be. Perhaps the villagers would say that she 'had slipped and drowned in the river too.'

As she made her way through the main hall she asked Anwen if she could have one of the flower braids that had been woven into her hair as a memento. Anwen gave it to her, and it smelled of something ancient and intoxicating.

The townspeople drifted out of the castle, and at exactly 11:50 p.m. the doors of Ragland Castle were closed.

CHAPTER NINE

WINN

When he was with her, he was happy. She was so easy to be around—so uncomplicated, so interesting, so smart, and so beautiful. He felt whole when he was with her. He felt like she was an extension of him and without her he would not be able to exist. She had taught him that you can only see things clearly with your heart; your heart is the only thing that allows you to give of yourself freely without question. She had taught him that you only care about the things that you spend time nurturing. He wanted to nurture Anwen for as long as he could. He would do whatever it took to make sure that she was at his side.

Winn knew that his father, Lord Blathaon, understood how much he loved Anwen, but because he could not change the laws that he governed the villagers by, Winn could never marry her. Anwen was a commoner. He could take her into his bed as a lover, but not as his wife. Anwen was too good for that, too chaste. Winn knew that she would never be with him unless it was done the right way.

The night he'd spent with Anwen in the castle was the beginning of something he could not explain. He was drawn to this woman for reasons that were unknown to him and that he would only understand in time. It went against all logical thinking, and it became an obsession to make sure that at some time during the day or night he got to see her, even if it was only just to catch her eye.

Each morning when he woke, after breakfast he had his duties to perform. He was expected to learn the skills of combat. There was a war being fought and he was expected to prepare himself in the skills of war to be able to defend his village. Defend his Anwen. The Mythrians were a brutal people who had landed on the shores of his homeland. Stories of their brutality had preceded them. Whilst he was sparring with his peers all he could think about was meeting Anwen at the stream or taking her deeper into the forest where her grandmother Teleri lived. He loved the time he spent with them. The villagers respected Teleri and Branwenn but were afraid of them, and it was whispered that they were witches.

CHAPTER TEN

Bronwen

The morning after the Day of Festivals, Anwen woke feeling ravenous. She had not eaten much the day before, and it had been an active day, what with the tug-o-war, the flower threading, and all the dancing. She smiled remembering the moments she had shared with Winn, moments no one else could take away from either of them. It was a chemistry that had surely been created by something powerful. She was amazed at just how special those moments had been. After all, she'd had great relationships with so many other people, but they paled in comparison. She was loved by everyone and in turn loved everyone. Yet there had always been something missing from her life. She could never really put her finger on what it was. She remembered her mother telling her something during one of their 'teaching days.' Branwen had told her that the most important lesson to learn about life was how we nurtured the relationships with those around us. She'd said that human frailty is measured by each person's ability to be able to continue forward after being damaged by the ravages of life's experiences.

She had told her that all of us are born with exactly the same chances in life. We all had equal ability to make something good happen or not. The number of days that we are given in which to complete this was predetermined, and how we chose to use those days could either take us forward to reaching true happiness and fulfilment or not. Her mother explained that we were given the tools with which to tackle this task, the task of being a 'great human being.' She said that if we only looked around and understood that we are all part of a chain—starting with the great oak tree to the deer under that oak to the man or animal who hunts that deer and then back to the carcass of that animal that feeds the soil to feed the tree, coming full circle. Without one the other cannot exist. As human beings we like to think that we are greater than the place we inhabit. She had looked sad and said that she wished more people understood. It was those people who didn't get this right in their lives that would then have to go forward into another until they eventually did.

She'd said, 'Remember, Anwen, have respect for nature and those people in the world around you, and this will help you grow as a person.'

Anwen did not realise just how complex this lesson could be. There were so many different people out there in the world—each person with his or her own personality—and there were those she really did not like to be around. Trying to learn from them was about as much fun as bathing in the stream at the beginning of winter. It left you feeling numb in lots of awkward places!

She dressed herself and went to put some water on the fire and make herself a hot milk. She would treat herself and put lots of honey in it. Then she would sit down to a bowl of porridge, again with lots of honey and perhaps some of the butter Teleri had made the day before, the one with the special herb in it (the one that made the butter taste sweet and aromatic). Teleri was so clever. She knew the art of making food taste more than delicious. She knew which herbs to use with which kind of meat, vegetables, or beverage to enhance your senses. Eating was not just something one had to do to stay alive. No, it was more than that in her household growing up. It was like a Day of Festivals twice a day, seven days a week!

As she was swallowing the last of the warmed milk there was a bang on the door. Lilybet, Braith's sister, was in a terrible state. She told Anwen that Bronwen had not returned home from the night before. They were calling the townsfolk to search the forest and surrounding area of the castle grounds.

Teleri told Anwen that she would not come since she did not think it was wise. She knowingly looked at Anwen and told her that she would be watching from afar and that if she was needed Anwen could call on her.

Anwen and Lilybet made off for the castle. They would have to pass through the forest since Teleri's home was on the other side of the stream in what was known as the untamed part of the forest.

The stream divided the forest into two parts. Not many people wandered too far into the untamed side. People were superstitious and created stories about things that they did not understand. Anwen liked it that way. She liked living on 'that' side of the stream. It was peaceful and beautiful and there were so many things that she had to learn about.

Anwen and Lilybet crossed the stream at a place where nature had created stepping stones. It was safe to cross most of the year. It was only when there had been a lot of rainfall that it became a bit tricky. Before they had died, Glendwyr and her brothers had fashioned a rope made from the vines that climbed the huge trees. It was so thick in some places that you had to use both hands to get a good grip.

As they passed over the middle part of the stream Anwen stopped dead in her tracks. The water was no longer crystal clear. She could not see the fish swimming around the stones beneath her. The water had become cloudy, and she didn't understand what she was looking at. She reached up to grab the vine to steady herself, and she stood perfectly still. She had been taught enough to know that she was about to experience something no one else in the village would ever come to accept and understand. She asked Lilybet to hold still and give her a moment. Lilybet knew enough to understand that Anwen was about to be shown something extraordinary.

Anwen took a deep breath and cleared her mind. She could hear her heart beating in her chest and the gentle trickle of the stream over the rocks. There was no other sound.

She looked down into the water and studied the swirl of cloudiness. She was being shown Bronwen leaving Ragland Castle. She could see her happy and smiling, chatting away merrily with two other girls. She saw her making her way towards the area that had been cleared and laid out for the women to relieve themselves. She saw her leave there and stop in her tracks. She could sense that she had been asked to turn around, and she now walked towards a figure standing in the line of the trees leading into the forest. Bronwen was smiling and seemed very happy. Anwen's heart stopped and the breath caught in the back of her throat as she saw Cedrick put his arm around her and move her into the thick of the trees.

Anwen looked to the sky. She took a deep breath and felt unsteady on her feet. She did not want to look back; she did not want to see this. She had 'seen' what Cedrick had done to Bronwen, and she knew it was not going to have a good outcome.

Lilybet reached forward and put her hand on Anwen's shoulder to steady her. The warmth from her hand gave Anwen the courage to look down and witness an attack that was so savage she lost her footing and her grip and she fell into the water. She sat in the water the chill of which slowed down the panicked beating of her heart.

Tears were rolling down her cheeks, and she felt empty inside. She felt the loss of that life. She felt the imbalance that had been created, that there was now a missing link in the chain. This life had been snuffed out before it had had the chance to find its purpose.

Lilybet was crouching next to her, trying to calm her and bring her to her feet. Anwen looked up at her face and reached out to pull herself up out of the water. She was wet from the waist down and would get really cold unless she managed to get dry quickly.

Lilybet suggested they go past her place that was on the way so she could change out of her wet clothes. Lilybet's older sister, Seren, could lend her something to wear. They made their way there in silence, Lilybet too afraid to ask Anwen what she had seen and Anwen was too afraid to put what she had seen into words. Speaking made it real.

She changed and thanked Lilybet's sister for the loan of her dress. As they passed through the thick of the wood in the tamed side of the forest, Anwen walked slower and slower. Her feet felt like lead, and as she approached the place where she knew she would find Bronwen she asked for Lilybet's hand. She did not want her to see what she knew would certainly be horrific.

She picked up the pace, and squeezing Lilybet's hand, she pulled her past that awful place through to the open field where the bonfire had been made.

The embers were still burning and the warmth from them could cook an egg. She saw Winn and Folant, the man who was appointed to watch over Winn. They were watching as the townsfolk all gathered around Bronwen's mother and father. She was their only child, and they were distressed. Winn asked Folant to tell them that they would do everything possible to bring their daughter back to them safe and sound. Lord Blathaon had given him charge of fifty men to help with the search.

Anwen walked up to Meirion, the missing girl's mother. The woman's face was pale. She was frail, unlike her daughter, who clearly had her father to thank for her size. Meirion's eyes were rimmed-red and her nose was red and Anwen could see that she had been crying for a long time. Meirion smiled at Anwen and put out her arms to hold her. As she took Anwen into her arms, Meirion felt calmed. Anwen had an 'aroma' about her. It was in her hair. It was a smell that she did not know but it made her feel safe and secure and for a brief moment she felt respite from the panicked pain she was feeling. She did not want to let Anwen go.

Winn approached the two women. He touched Meirion gently on the shoulder and she stepped back from Anwen. He asked if he could talk to Anwen and offered her husband a chair and some mead from the night before.

Anwen walked with Winn so she was not within earshot of the couple or the townsfolk. She asked Lilybet to stay with Bronwen's parents.

Winn could tell by the look on Anwen's face that she was very upset by something. These were not the circumstances that he wanted to have his next meeting with her. She was so beautiful and it was so hard to concentrate on the situation that they were all facing. He could 'smell' that strange aroma again it was in her hair for when the wind caught her hair the smell was stronger and it was very hard not to pull her close and kiss her. He could tell she'd been crying and although her cheeks were flushed her face was an unhealthy white.

She moved away from him and sat down on a stone bench. It was a wonderful spot that overlooked the river that ran past the castle. The vast expanse of the forest lay before her like a lush green carpet. So dense was the forest that unless you knew the trees as if they were familiar friends, one could get lost. She regained her composure and took a deep breath. She caught Winn's scent, but her heart was sore with the reality of her discovery of the body. She felt nauseous and faint.

She looked up at him and her eyes filled with tears again. Biting her bottom lip she choked back the tears and tried in the most sensible way to tell this lord that she knew where Bronwen could be found and that she also knew her demise and the identity of the one who had caused it. She realised that the way in which she related her story could cause her to end up in the same unfortunate state as her beloved family: burnt to ashes. As she looked at Winn, though, she had a glimpse of an ancient reasoning. She could tell that he too understood that not all things were easily explained and that there were things of this world that one would never fully comprehend. As a lord, she knew he would protect her. She hoped he would.

She told him that although they had just met, she needed him to know that he could trust that she was sound of mind. That she came from a very old family, a family that was honest and true and pure, and that her family had had certain gifts bestowed upon them, including the gift of healing, the gift of knowledge, and the gift of 'sight.'

Winn encouraged her to continue. Anwen explained that she lived on the other side of the stream in the untamed forest. She noted his surprise. She explained that the river was not only a source of life for the village but a mystical place of knowledge and healing. She tried to explain how she had been shown a vision in the waters of the river. It had shown her that Bronwen was stuffed into the hollow of a dead oak and that she had been brutally attacked, and the identity of the attacker had been made clear.

Without a single hesitation Winn turned to call Folant to send out a party of men to the hollow tree. Anwen told him that she would go with them but that once they discovered the body, she would leave and go back home. She did not want the people of the village to know how they had found her.

So Winn sent Folant back to the bonfire and asked him to disperse the crowd and start their search. Winn took Anwen's hand and followed her into the thick of the forest, past the area where the ladies lean-to had been erected, through an opening where a large tree lay across the forest floor.

He noticed that no leaves covered the ground. The earth had been disturbed and scuffed. He noticed blood, and he found shreds of Bronwen's clothing littered about.

Anwen stood at the opening of the line of trees. She had no desire to go any closer. She pointed to the tree and urged Winn to move to the bottom of the tree. There Winn found Bronwen. Or what was left of her. She had been eaten by wolves and only the top half of her body remained. He asked Anwen to turn around, and he pulled her remains from the tree. Her hair was matted with leaves and her face was blue. Her eyes bulged out of their sockets, and there was a bruising around her neck. He felt nauseous and sad, and he saw that one nipple was missing; it looked like it had been bitten off, for there were teeth marks on the soft white flesh of her breast. He understood that she had obviously been the victim of a terrible assault. The human being who had attacked her had been brutal and savage and it was hard for him to imagine that such a person could be living amongst the people of his father's village.

He called his men to gently place her on a stretcher they had made from blankets and sticks and to cover her and take her around to the back entrance of the castle. He instructed them to take her down into the undercroft and store her body there whilst Folant could send for the undertaker to craft a coffin for her remains. To make sure that it was a full length coffin. He also instructed them to tell the undertaker that they were to make sure that she was dressed beautifully and to create an illusion that she was not just half a cadaver. Her parents could not find peace with the world knowing that their daughter was ravaged as well as murdered. Winn thanked Anwen and saw her on her way and went back to the bonfire to break the news to Bronwen's parents.

The shrill of Meirion's grief echoed throughout the forest, bouncing off the trees like an arrow finding its resting place deep in Anwen's heart.

From the shadows, Cedrick was watching. He saw Winn discover Bronwen's body and thought he should have let out the pigs—the wolves had not done a thorough job. Anwen could not do this to him.

CHAPTER ELEVEN

Winn

Some weeks later, as Winn was in the forest close to Teleris's home, he heard Anwen crying softly as he came around the corner. She was lying under the tree where they had met. She was bruised and bleeding. His heart was racing as the anger welled up inside him like a tidal wave. As he knelt beside her he saw the hand marks around her neck. Her beautiful hair was matted and damp from tears. He remembered the corpse of Bronwen, as he gathered Anwen to him he looked into her big brown eyes, she whispered 'Cedrick' and he saw her soul fading . . .

He took in a deep breath. Why? What had happened? Who could have done this? His beautiful Anwen . . . . Time as he perceived it seemed to slow down. His senses became razor sharp. He could hear his heart beating—he could hear Anwen's faint breathing. The dust particles hung in the air suspended in the moment. He could hear people running through the forest laughing and shouting. He could smell his Anwen—her smell, that one of cooked potatoes, honey, and earth—only this time it was tainted with the smell of blood, the rancour of another man—maybe more—and the smell of fear and sweat. He knew he had to find 'them.'

The forest would hide her, surround her in the mist until he could come back and take her to safety, take her back and let Teleri wash away the spoils of this deed with the herbs and ointments she had taught him about.

He lifted her and hid her deeper inside the forest. He covered her with leaves and whispered to the spirit of the forest to care for her whilst he was way. He kissed her gently on the lips and lingered for a moment to see that she was still breathing. He whispered, 'Rwy'n dy gari di.'(I love you). Then he turned and ran in the direction of the noise.

As his feet hit the ground faster and faster his mind drifted back to the day before he and Anwen had met by the stream. She had suggested they go fishing. She had boasted that since she could talk to Mother Nature, she could almost 'will' a fish onto her hook. He remembered how her hair tickled his face and how it fell softly down her back onto his chest and groin. It felt smooth and silky and he liked the way the light reflected off its blackness. She had been so happy, laughing and singing, teasing him about how she wondered if her 'knight' knew how to make a fire to cook their catch of the day.

The forest seemed to fade into obscurity as he ran. The noise that he was following was getting fainter and he had to run harder to not lose the sounds. He remembered how after cooking the fish Anwen had gone down to the stream to wash her hands. She looked so beautiful squatting by the edge of the water, totally oblivious to the fact that 'ladies' do not squat. Her dress was hoisted up over her knees. Her beautiful long legs were well toned. He could tell that she had worked hard in her life. She had not been a lady of leisure. He remembered how he had been spellbound as she had cupped some water and lifted her long black hair to wash the back of her neck and the top of her ample bosom. Just at that moment she had looked up to catch him watching her, and he remembered how she had met his gaze. Her eyes were the window to her soul, and he had felt like he was going to drown when he looked at her. It had made his heart race and the blood rise from his toes to the top of his head. He felt like she was burning a hole through him, as only she could do.

Anwen's words resonated in his heart as he tried to conceptualise their meaning. She had told him that her love was as vast and as deep as an ocean. It ebbed and flowed ever constant but was always changing. She said that unless it had a beach it could lap upon, its beauty and worth was lost. Unless it had a beach to reach out and caress, the love would be lost. She needed him to be her beach. To always be there to absorb her soul. He knew this to be an infinite truth of old and that life as he understood it could never change its meaning.

He was jolted from this memory by a loud thud. Up ahead he could see those he had been pursuing. These were the demons who had defiled this gentle creature who had come into his life and made him complete. There were four of them, Cedrick and his crew.

Winn rested for a moment to catch his breath. He was sweating profusely and couldn't contain his anger. He knew that he had to allow himself time—time to gather his thoughts and time to ask for help, Anwen's help. For he knew she was with him. He could feel her close.

Cedrick and his brothers had just killed a deer and were busy skinning and gutting it. This would allow him the time to plan his revenge. The moment would present itself, of that he was certain.

Illustrated by Vanessa Jones 2012

CHAPTER TWELVE

By the time he got back to the place he had left Anwen it was twilight, that time of day when the mist creeps in and fills the space where sunlight had once been. He remembered her telling him it was a magical time, a time of day when reality and myth seemed to meld into one and it was difficult to know what was real and what was not. He smelled the forest as it came alive with things that did not exist during the light of day. He was suddenly filled with an emptiness that gripped his heart and grew like a fungus throughout his body. He became aware that he could not see her. She was not where he had left her. The mist shifted and he caught the scent of her. Perhaps she had regained consciousness and had moved farther into the forest to protect herself.

Winn stood and steadied himself. In the way she had shown him he closed his eyes and opened his mind, so allowing him to sharpen his senses. The silence was deafening, and he panicked because he could not focus. He spread his legs further apart to steady himself and prevent himself from fainting and filled his lungs with the air around him. The mist moved closer to his body, and for a moment he felt claustrophobic.

Then he heard her voice. He opened his eyes and searched through the mist to try to figure which direction it was coming from. What he believed he saw was not Anwen but a girl who looked like her. Her skin was olive in complexion and her eyes were darker than Anwen's, if that was possible. She was naked to the waist. He was filled with the same love he felt for Anwen. Somehow he knew this woman.

He knew her in a way that completed him, and yet she was like no other thing he had ever seen before. He stepped forward to speak to her, but as he opened his mouth she vanished.

He felt something brush the back of his neck. Winn turned, and an apparition in the form of his Anwen was before him. Her skin was paler though, and he struggled to move—her form was moving in and out of the mist. He could not reach out and touch her, and he could not speak. All he could do was watch. His feet felt like lead. He had a faint awareness of the sweet smell of something she had once shown him. He realised it was the smoke from the cipbar bush. Perhaps the apparition he was seeing was nothing more than a product of this, he thought.

He shook his head and tried to focus. He caught a flicker of light and advanced towards it. As he moved it felt like he was passing down a tunnel of time. He heard strange sounds and a strange language. He kept moving towards the light.

He came through the thickness into an opening in the forest where Anwen and Teleri were seated around a fire Teleri was lovingly holding Anwen and singing gently to her—a song of healing. The smoke from the leaves of the cipbar bush was strong and it caught in the back of his throat, but he knew that it was needed to calm her down and allow her body and mind the time to heal itself. He could see that her physical wounds were not life-threatening. She was bruised and had a few minor flesh wounds.

It was the wounds to her mind that he could not see. He needed to know what had happened.

Teleri looked up and saw him and beckoned him to come and sit beside them. 'We've been waiting for you,' she said. 'It's important that you are here as we ask Anwen to go back and show us what Cedrick and his brothers have done. She will need you by her side as she walks us through the chain of events. It is important that she feels safe at all times.'

CHAPTER THIRTEEN

Anwen

Anwen could not look at Winn in the same way after that day. She felt as though he could no longer see 'her' but the discarded shell of something once sweet and sacred. Cedrick had taken the 'sweet and sacred' in a way that she could never have expected. Like a nut he had crushed her outer shell and ravaged the very essence of that which Mother Nature held in the highest regard, the source of human life in its purest form. The greatest gift entrusted to a woman for all human kind was the ability to create a life. He used it and discarded it.

Up to that point in her life she had achieved almost everything her heart had desired. She had learnt the teachings her mother had asked her grandmother to continue with, and Anwen had advanced even further. The shadows of ancient time had taken her into their understanding, and there were things that she had been shown and things that she had learnt that Teleri could not comprehend even at her advanced age. Anwen's understanding had transcended into another realm because of who she had become. Anwen had come to understand that her innocence and her maidenhood could not have just been given to any man. If she had done this she would not have been able to achieve the level of understanding that she had achieved.

As beautiful as Anwen was, her beauty within remained intact. She had grown so beautiful that she knew that she would not be able to stop the course of nature. The suitors were lining up at her doorway, men coming from distant villages just for the chance to win her affections. Up to that day, Anwen had felt proud that she had learnt to appreciate those people around her for who they were and what they could teach her. She had studied the forest and its creatures and mysteries and learnt the secrets therein. She had been able to do so because she was pure, pure within and pure without. Not even those within the village who called her a witch could do so to her face since within their very being they knew it was an ignorant word.

Winn carried her home and lay her on her bed. He had never been in her room before. Most of his time with her and her grandmother had been spent in the forest. Teleri and Anwen showed him things that he would never have believed if he had not seen them for himself.

Her room was small but illuminated by a large round window. The view showed him Ragland Castle in the far distance, the tamed forest, the river within, and the untamed forest opening into a small clearing. It was as if they were in fact on top of a mountain. The room was abundant with fragrant flowers and beautiful stones, including ones he had helped Anwen seek out from deep within the forest and from the shores of the river. Anwen taught him that these stones held the colours of all living things, including human beings and that it was up to each person to find his own aura and guard it and keep it in its purest form. She told him that each person had their own unique colour and that it was up to each person to make sure life's experiences did not 'muddy' its pureness. For the minute you allowed the mixing of colours within your aura you would never again be able to get it back. Spoilt for all eternity and only when you are reborn do we get the chance to once again be a clean and pure spirit.

He had not seen Anwen's stone. She had told him she'd found hers. The river had given it to her only a week before. He longed to see what it looked like and hoped that one day he would be lucky enough to find his stone and in so doing be able to protect his aura and keep it clean. He wasn't even sure that he had not already damaged the pureness of its colour.

Anwen watched him as he walked around her room, touching the things that she had laid about in such a precise way. She could read his thoughts, and as he turned to look at her she said, 'You will find your stone soon; you still have time, for your aura is not yet damaged.'

He came over to the side of her bed and knelt down; he took her hand in his. How could this be, for he had taken a human life on more than one occasion?

Anwen told him that nature gives us the tools to protect ourselves and guard that which is most sacred to us.

As she told him this he felt the walls of the room close in on him, for he knew he had failed. He had not protected her from the abomination that was Cedrick. He had been told the stories of how throughout their lives he had stalked her. He should have known that one such as Cedrick would not give up until he had taken what it was that he wanted.

Teleri came into the room holding a bowl with steaming water. In it she placed the ointment that Winn knew to be so familiar. Next she gathered some of the flowers from the room and placed them in the bowl. She took a lock of hair from Anwen and asked her for her stone. Winn turned away when Teleri found it and placed it in the water. He did not want to look. It was not his to see and he had not been given permission to do so. Teleri laid the bowl in front of the window and came and sat beside her granddaughter. She asked Winn to wait outside whilst she washed Anwen's body clean after which he would be requested to come back in.

After what seemed like a lifetime Teleri called him back inside. Anwen was dressed in a fresh nightgown, and her hair had been brushed and oiled with the ointment. She was so incredibly beautiful. Her big brown eyes however were changed. The flame that had once burned within them was no longer there, and it took all of his willpower to smile and reassure her that everything was going to be good again. His heart was breaking and the rage welled up inside him again like a bonfire out of control. Teleri told him that he would be required to lie next to Anwen and hold her close, that as difficult as it would become he had to promise not to let her go.

Anwen lay down, and as Winn moved onto the bed next to her she felt as if her heart was going to break. This is not how it was meant to be. This beautiful man was here by her side but not in the manner in which she had dreamed. She could smell him and she inhaled him into her inner being—her heartbeat slowed and she calmed herself. She moved onto her side and reached her arm across his chest. She moved her leg over his body across his legs and placed her head on his chest. She heard his heart beating and felt his breath on her face.

Winn placed both of his arms around her and held her tight. Anwen closed her eyes and exhaled. She lay there drawing on his strength, feeling his heartbeat, smelling him close. She felt the warmth of his body and slowly began to drift off into a deep sleep. Her breathing became so faint that at one point Winn thought that she had died. But he did as he had been told and held on to her and never let her go.

He opened his eyes and saw that by the window the bowl that Teleri had placed there was emitting a bluish hue, an iridescent light. As the light grew stronger Anwen began to tell the story of what had happened.

'I'd gone down to the river to gather water. I was filling the bucket and was aware that I was being watched. I knew it was Cedrick—apart from the fact that I could "sense" his presence, since Bronwen's death he had vowed to watch me even closer for causing him so much ridicule.' Anwen sighed and thought, *He's been watching me for years now, after all.* He was angry that although nothing had been proven, for it was only Anwen's 'vision' that revealed the murderer, his family had been shamed and he had been outcast from the village as a respectable member of the community.

'Cedrick told me that he knew it was my fault because I had told Winn what I had seen that day in the river. As he came closer he told me that he had loved me his whole life and that in his opinion I had never acknowledged him. I watched him move towards me like he was floating on air. I couldn't get away from him. As he reached out to grab me I managed to hit him across his face and threw him off balance. I turned and ran and hoped that I would make it into the thick of the untamed forest in time to hide. Unfortunately, he had anticipated I would go in that direction and his brothers lay in the bushes waiting for me. They caught me, and between the four of them they carried me into the thick of the forest. I couldn't kick or shake them free.

'Cedrick ripped the talisman from around my neck, and the memory of the years of his lecherous glances, his lewd remarks, and his inappropriate behaviour were too much to bear. I knew then what he intended to do to me, and I felt completely defeated. Without the strength of the talisman I could offer no resistance. I had spent all those years protecting something that was so precious to me and it would now be taken from me, by this man I despised, and yet had treated with respect as I had been taught to. And so as they laid me on the ground I stopped struggling and turned to face the reality that was moving towards me like a tidal wave. Helpless in its path, I could do nothing more than face it head on.

'As I lay there, I looked up. Standing over me was that woman I told you about that night at the Day of Festivals. She appeared out of nowhere, and it seemed that only I could see her. She is not of this time. Her skin is olive in complexion and her eyes are almost black in colour. She held her hand out to me and it was as though I had stepped out of my body. I seemed to be standing next to her looking at myself. I stood with her as Cedrick and his brothers took from me that which I have held so sacred. I saw myself lying there with no expression on my face, just tears rolling down my cheeks. This woman beside me stepped between me and my physical self and she placed her one hand over my heart and another over my eyes. As she touched me I felt warmth spread from within my chest. It moved through my body till I felt as though I was lying in a hot tub of water. As she covered my eyes I saw the most beautiful sight I have ever seen. I saw those magnificent castles (the ones I told you that I had seen at the 'Day of Festivals'), the ones that pointed to the sky. A river ran past, a magnificent river. It was wide and deep and it seemed to shimmer like a thousand stars on a clear night. It had a presence, a soul and tranquillity, one such as I have only experienced on a similar level with our river but on a smaller scale. On each side of the banks of this river was a lush fertile land. I saw people who looked just as she did their bodies naked to the waist. The olive colour of their flesh was oiled and smooth. They all had black hair and dark eyes like she. They were threshing a crop that they had reaped and they were singing an ancient song in a language I did not understand. The sound of it resonated off the water and sent a shrill through my very being. She led me to the banks of the river and sat me down. She handed me a goblet of some sort and encouraged me to drink it. As it hit my stomach I felt a burning within that was so great. I dropped the goblet and clutched at my belly. As I did this I caught a glimpse of Cedrick violating my physical self and I thought that at this point I was going to lose my mind. This woman drew me close to her body and the pain subsided and I was aware once again of the beautiful river in front of me. Its waters gently lapping around my feet cool against my warm skin.

'The sound of singing became louder. This ethereal creature slipped into the water and pulled me in with her. The weight of my body was swallowed by the silky water, and I felt like I was floating. She moved behind me and put her arms around my body. I felt at peace, safe and untouchable.

'I don't know for how long I remained in that river but after some time she took my hand, and I found that we were standing once again in the forest. I saw Cedrick and his brothers laughing and joking with each other. I saw my shell lying there broken and dirtied. She took my face in her hands and kissed my mouth, her breath smelt sweet and pure. I closed my eyes, and when I opened them I was flesh once again. I turned my head and saw Cedrick and his brothers running off into the forest. I lay there feeling like a tree had fallen on my body. It was then that I saw you, Winn. I felt you pick me up and take me deep into the forest where, as I lay in the cool of the darkness, I heard you run off into the forest in the direction of my attackers.'

Winn was holding Anwen close, tears burning his cheeks. His body was shaking and he wanted to scream. He wanted to run and keep running. As he lay there he thought of how he had tracked Cedrick and his brothers. Killing them would not be justice enough for this heinous crime.

Teleri saw his anguish and left the room.

Anwen sat up and slipped off the bed. She stood over him, watching his body quivering as he quietly sobbed. She pulled him up and held him close. She held him close until the racing of his heart beat in time with hers. Anwen felt loved and safe and surprisingly calm. She kissed him gently on his neck and asked him to leave. She was very tired and desperately needed to sleep.

Teleri came into the room and took him by the arm, led him out, thanked him, and told him to come back the next day. After Winn left, Anwen collapsed on the bed and cried herself to sleep.

CHAPTER FOURTEEN

Sekhet

As the dawn broke and as she opened her eyes, her mind was washed clean and felt fresh. She could hear Teleri making the fire and for a few seconds the horror of the day before no longer existed. As the memory returned she felt the pain that her body had endured. Her heart felt heavy in her chest. How would she be able to be whole again, happy again, free again of this weight that had landed on her like a mountain?

Teleri came into the room. Her face had aged in the night, Anwen thought, but she smiled and handed her a hot cup of milk with honey. She spoke softly but sternly and told Anwen that no matter how difficult she thought this lesson was, she would recover. Anwen was, after all, a 'child of nature' and an extraordinary human being who had the ability to give love and heal others. She would find the strength to heal herself. It was just that she did not know how she could accept the fate that life had dealt her. Her beautiful Winn would not be hers in the way she had hoped for. Cedrick's assault was nothing in comparison to the reality of the fact that she could no longer be Winn's wife.

She got up and washed and dressed herself and made her way to the kitchen for something to eat. She knew that once she had something in her stomach she would feel better.

After breakfast Anwen decided she would take a walk down to the river, the place that had given her so much over her time on this Earth. She loved being by the river. It calmed her spirit and helped her focus and see things as they should be seen. She needed to have time there to be able to adjust to the events of the past two days. She needed to find the time to be quiet and allow Mother Nature to show her what it is that she must do, and why it was that she should have had to endure this brutal attack after she had been so careful to protect herself from harm. She had been studious and done everything asked of her, and just when she had found the love of her life this one precious thing was taken from her.

As she made her way down to the river she contemplated the ramifications of such an attack. Whilst she knew it was impossible that she could have ever been wed to Winn, she had always secretly hoped that the law would change or that Winn wouldn't care about his status in the community and marry her anyway.

But this new development meant that she was no longer 'pure', and she felt sure that this fact in itself would make her even more of an outcast amongst her community. The people of the Village always found it difficult to 'label' her as 'different' they could never quite bring themselves to calling her a witch because she was such an 'extra' ordinary being, but now with this she knew that the looks she would be getting would be of a very different kind. She was crying by the time she reached the river. She reached the spot where the stepping stones were, the place where her darling father and brothers had made the vine to cross. She looked around to make sure no one was watching and continued forward about forty steps, where right on the river bank was a massive tree, the base of which was almost as big as a small house. A great vine ran down the tree.

Anwen looked up and marvelled at the profound greatness of this massive old tree; it should surely be hundreds of years old. It reached up and up and she could not see the top. She always wished she could climb it. This is where her brother had cut a piece of the vine from. It was so thick in some places that it had totally concealed a hole within the base of the tree. She checked once more that no one was watching and pushed the vines aside and went into its cavity.

It smelled of mushrooms and moss and another smell. It was a sweet smell and she knew that this is where the cipbar bush grew amongst many other special plants that she used to create the healing ointments she made and the ointment that she used to comb through her hair. It was serene and ethereal and she felt like she had stepped through the door of time to a place where man and nature were one. This was the place that only just recently she had learnt her greatest lesson, the place where she had been given a gift that neither her mother nor grandmother had been given, the gift of being able to 'hear' nature and understand what it was trying to say. As a farmer her father could have been a very successful man had she had this gift whilst he was alive. She was able to understand why the leaves on the different trees and shrubs died when they did, at different times. Why certain things only grew in certain places and what was needed to allow them to thrive. She had learnt that nature calls out and man did not listen, often destroying the very thing necessary for human survival.

She sat down and made a small fire and placed upon it the leaves of the cipbar bush. As the smoke began to fill the air around her, she placed her shawl down on the moss and sat cross-legged in front of the fire. It was only a small fire but it cast a light within the great blackness inside the tree. As she inhaled the smoke and looked around, she looked up and noticed that it looked as though someone had taken the stars from the night sky and stuck them all over the walls of this secret place. For as far as her eye could see there was a shimmering like a million diamonds. She realised that perhaps it was just the gum of the bark that had formed in such a way over the hundreds of years this tree had stood. It was truly beautiful, and she marvelled again at the magnificence of nature.

She was stalling now, for the questions she needed to ask were too painful and she did not know if she had the strength to cope with anything more. Anwen steadied herself, took a deep breath, and closed her eyes. She thought about where she was, how beautiful it was, and the fact that here within the belly of this great tree no one could harm her. Her heart slowed down and her mind opened.

As she opened her eyes, sitting on the opposite side of the fire was the woman from her visions. She was seated just as Anwen was, a mirror image of her. The only thing that was different was the expression on her face. She was smiling, and her incredibly big dark eyes were filled with love and understanding. Anwen sat and marvelled at her beauty. When the woman spoke, her voice seemed to caress Anwen's body. The tone of her voice was like nothing she had ever heard before. It was rich and thick and yet incredibly clear.

She looked at Anwen and said, 'My name is Sekhet, and I am here to guide and protect you. Do not be afraid. You have seen me before and you know who I am. I have not spoken to you before since you were not ready to hear my voice and you would not have been able to understand me. Once you walked the halls of my home, that time you glanced into the water on your day of festivals, but you did not understand, and again when I came to keep you safe and took you to the River of my home. You did not understand the singing of my people. Last night whilst you slept your grandmother filled a bowl with water, and your stone and other things allowed the cobwebs to be cleared from your head and open your ears. You are an extraordinary woman, Anwen, and you have been chosen to do many wonderful things in your lifetime. I know that your heart is breaking right now and that you cannot comprehend the events of the past few days. It is too complicated for me to explain to you but I am here to try and show you what it is that you now have to do and what is expected of you.

'I come from a land far away, Anwen, from a time far away. Just as I sit opposite you, like your reflection, so it is that we are linked, for I am you and you are me. I had a life such as yours and the man I loved is the very same that you love. All will be made clear to you, but there are greater things at hand and there is something that you need to know. I know the answer to the question that sits heavy on your heart: "Am I with child?" The answer to this is yes, you are'.

As she said these words Anwen's heart froze and swelled within her chest. She felt as though she was going to faint. She reached out her hand and Sekhet mirrored her action, their hands meeting midair. The flesh of her hand was warm and soothing. She felt like she had reached up and touched the sun and the warmth filled her body and mind and she felt very relaxed.

Sekhet continued. 'The child within your belly will come to bring you great joy. For as brutal as was the attack on you, she is the mirrored opposite. We are taught that only bad things come from bad things and this is often so. But you, Anwen, are special, for you have the ability to change the course of nature. You have been given the ability to create something beautiful from something ugly. From this day forward the memory of how the child came to be within you will fade, and indeed each time you give it thought it allows the poison within you to be made pure and clean. As she continues to grow she will fill you with an incredible joy. You will come to understand that there is life within your belly and you will marvel at the wonder of it all.

'There is much you will have to endure, and the direction of your life is forever changed. The dream you have for yourself will come in a different form, and although it is not the one you had wished for, it will suffice. You have to accept that you cannot change what has happened and you cannot explain the evil that lies within the hearts of mankind. You will find peace in knowing that by allowing yourself to love this child you will be allowing something wonderful for her and you will be rewarded and given the chance to grow and learn.'

Sekhet removed her hand from Anwen's and untied a small bag from around her waist. She handed the bag to Anwen and told her to open it.

She tipped the contents of the bag out into her hand and saw that it was a stone, such as she had never seen before. It was of every colour under the sun and was streaked with gold and silver.

Sekhet said, 'This is my stone, and I am giving it to you. You are to keep it safe, and when your daughter is born you are to place it around her neck.'

Anwen put the stone back into the bag and put it inside the bodice of her frock close to her heart.

'Now', said Sekhet, 'the last and most important task of all. You have to promise me that you will continue to remain chaste, that you will not be tempted to allow your heart to reach out to Winn. That you will not be tempted to be drawn to be with him, for if you do you will forever change the course of your life and that of your child. You will think that you have found incredible happiness with him, but I can assure you that you would be very wrong. The pain you endured with Cedrick will be nothing in comparison to the pain you will endure if you allow Winn to woo you. Be strong and steadfast, and if you feel your resistance is low I am here to help you. Reach for my stone and it will give you strength. There is something that will be revealed to you but I am not permitted to tell you at this moment in time. I am permitted to tell you, though, that one day you will be with him and when you are it will be a life such as you can imagine. The happiness you will have will be everlasting and eternal. You have already been taught that the meaning of our existence is within our relationships with others. Accept your destiny with grace.'

Anwen stood up, as did Sekhet. The beautiful woman reached out as Anwen did and they embraced. Two hearts beating in time, two halves of a whole being, two people, and one soul.

The air around Anwen grew cold, and she was aware that the fire had gone out and the stars in her world had disappeared. She sat in the darkness for some time contemplating what had just happened. She felt strangely comforted and restored. She reached down and held her belly and felt the warmth within, felt the life within her growing. She remembered how it got there and it tore at her heart but she could not quite remember how she had come to be in that place where it happened.

She walked to the entrance of the hole in the tree and stepped into the dappled light within the forest. The river was flowing, the birds were singing, and she felt as though she had the power to change the world as she knew it to be.

CHAPTER FIFTEEN

She made her way back up to the house. She saw Teleri standing by the doorway looking anxious, for she had been gone a long while. Teleri's face broke into a smile and she came down to meet her. She gathered her beautiful granddaughter within her arms and held her tight. Teleri was always astounded at Anwen's essence and it seemed to radiate through her eyes. She knew where she would have gone but did not know what had been revealed, for Teleri had not been given the same gifts as her granddaughter had.

Teleri said, 'Come, my darling child, I have prepared your favourite meal, and you will have a visitor to call on you shortly.'

Winn had been disappointed when he'd called on Anwen that morning. Teleri had told him to return that evening and it had been the longest day in his life. As he came up the hill he saw Anwen and Teleri walking hand in hand returning home. His heart was filled with love for this incredibly brave woman who had completely won his heart and soul. He vowed to love and protect her from that moment on till the day he died. He wondered how she had managed the day without his support and what frame of mind she would be in tonight.

He knew that whatever she had to say to him would be okay and he would do anything she needed him to do . . .

They spent the evening sitting around the table enjoying a wonderful meal. Winn was always so surprised that the food that was served in this house was always so much better than what he ate in his castle, with all the servants at his beck and call. It was the herbs and secret seasonings that made Teleri's food so special. They always seemed so exotic and so different. He especially loved the meal that Teleri had prepared this evening. It was a stew but it had what looked like some kind of vegetable in it that was hot on the tongue. He loved the way it burnt and made his eyes stream and his nose run.

Winn noted how different Anwen looked this evening. Her resolve to overcome filled his heart with love. Nothing she ever did or could ever say would make him feel any different about her. He loved her and that was that. From the time he made eye contact with her, the earth felt like it had literally moved from under him and he felt as though he already knew everything about her. The time that they had spent together was never awkward or forced. The quiet moments were never uncomfortable. Their relationship was like the ocean tide, one moving in and the other moving out. It just was, it just happened and it was so right.

Anwen looked up and saw him watching her. She met his stare and knew immediately what he was thinking. They seemed to be able to do that too.

Whenever one or the other was feeling sad or needed help they both knew it to be and took it as a message to come to one another's aid. As she looked into his eyes she felt so safe, so loved, and so complete. She remembered her day and the revelation that had been made known to her, and she could not hold his stare. She looked away and her eyes welled up with tears.

Winn didn't understand what she was thinking but took it upon himself to believe that it was Cedrick. He stood up and started pacing. There was so much rage within him and he knew that he needed to find a way to vent it. He sat back down and decided to tell Anwen what had become of Cedrick and his brothers. He felt that she should know although he knew she would not want to hear.

He began by telling her that he needed her to understand that he had never done anything like this before and asked her for her forgiveness. He told her there was no way possible that he could not have acted as he had. There was a force within him that seemed to be driving him and he could not resist.

Winn told her that after he left her he had tracked Cedrick and his brothers down. They had been hunting and had just killed a deer and were skinning it. He could not imagine how they had gone from defiling her to killing another helpless creature.

He had stood there for a time to calm himself and felt as though she was with him. He looked up at Anwen and she nodded in acknowledgment. He then told her that he had said the prayer that she had taught him, the one of old, the one calling on Mother Nature to help him protect that which belongs to her.

He stepped forward and noted that Cedrick and his brothers were crazed and their eyes were ablaze with sheer wickedness. As he approached them, the four of them had turned to face him, very ready for another killing encounter! At that point he felt that the outcome might end in his demise but he would certainly not go down without a fight, and as long as he took Cedrick he did not worry about the others. What transpired was a mystery to him, and he hoped Teleri and Anwen would be able to explain it.

Winn told them that when he saw the scratches that Anwen had made on the face of her attacker it acted like a trigger within him. Cedrick was shouting to his brothers, mocking Winn. As he moved forward Winn felt a wind blowing behind him. It was moving through the trees at a great speed. As it came closer to the spot they were, it brought with it all the debris on the forest floor, creating a spiral of leaves, twigs, and such. He had only glanced back once to see this and it somehow spurred him forward.

He ran at Cedrick and as he knocked him down it was as though his body was made of rock. It felt as though he possessed the strength of forty men. Cedrick was not a big man, certainly not as big as Winn. Winn was taller and finely chiselled. Cedrick was shorter and stout. As he hit Cedrick he knocked all the air out of his lungs. Cedrick's brothers had been shouting at Cedrick, telling him that 'the witch' had sent her army to get them! They were cavorting and cackling like a pack of scavengers, till they heard the wind. They looked up and saw the tunnel of wind coming at them out of nowhere, leaves and debris flying all over. The air was cold and the sky grew dark. Winn was not sure what had made them turn and run, but run they did, and he was left with Cedrick cursing and shouting for his brothers to come back.

Winn rolled off Cedrick and stood up. Cedrick crawled away looking for his knife. When he had located it he stood up and ran at Winn.

At that moment Winn knew that what he had to do was out of his hands. The wind was howling around them and it was difficult to be heard. He ran at Cedrick and as he cut into Cedrick he could hear Anwen's cries. He saw how

Cedrick had thrown her down to the ground to the cheers of his brothers. Winn felt his knife hit bone as it went through Cedrick's breastbone and hit his heart. Cedrick stopped in his tracks. Spit and bile oozed from his mouth.

Winn quietly uttered that he would leave him for the wolves and as Cedrick's blood hit the ground, Mother Nature took her revenge. A thistle bush sprouted. It was instantaneous. As Cedrick hit the ground, the earth seemed to sigh.

What he did next he did not tell the two women who were sitting holding each other. Both were crying. Winn could not tell them that he had then cut the tie to Cedrick's trousers and taken his manhood in his hand. As the life was draining from Cedrick's heart Winn cut his manhood off and shoved it in his mouth. 'That is for Anwen', he'd said. 'Your brothers will get the same treatment.'

The wind died down, and by the time it was all over there was not a breath of air. Not a sound was heard and the sky was clear. He could not explain the phenomena and could not explain where, at that point, the tree line of the forest lit up with what seemed like a hundred yellow eyes. The wolves stepped out from their hiding place and moved towards him. As Winn backed away he saw them descend upon Cedrick's body, tearing it limb from limb, and within a matter of minutes there was nothing left of him. Not even the clothes he had worn.

What had become of the three brothers was still not discovered. No one had seen or heard from them since.

Teleri stood up and moved over to him. She took his face in her hands and kissed him on his brow.

Anwen moved over to him. She took his face in her hands and kissed him on both of his eyelids. Then, for the first time since they had met, she kissed him on his mouth.

As she held his mouth to hers Winn carefully stood up and put his arms around her. She continued to hold him in that kiss until they both could no longer hold their breath.

Anwen then let his face go and stepped back from him. He was much taller, and she needed to step back to be able to see him properly. This was the man she believed she had loved her whole life. This was the man she felt she would love for all eternity. There was nothing more pure and true and righteous. There was no foul deed or act that could defile it. There was no person or persons who could change it. It just was. She felt lightheaded and strange and the longing within her body was immense.

Winn mirrored this and he felt unsteady on his feet. He longed for her on so many levels. He wanted to consume her. He wanted to drink her in, and he stepped forward and drew her close to his chest. As he held her he breathed her in, and it was as though time stood still. They both held the embrace, too afraid to shatter the moment. It felt as though finally this was the only place they should be. They felt complete, too afraid that if they did break the embrace they would never again be able to reunite.

Teleri moved forward and gently pulled them apart. No words were spoken. Winn looked at Anwen and he backed out of the house, never letting his gaze leave her face.

Anwen fell to the floor after he'd ridden away and let out a wail of anguish at the top of her lungs. It was filled with sadness, frustration, and longing.

Teleri pulled on her shawl and moved out into the night, leaving her granddaughter to face her emotion and grief in private.

CHAPTER SIXTEEN

Some months into Anwen's pregnancy . . .

Anwen reached the stage that when she woke, the first thing that came to mind was no longer *how* she had ended up with child but instead, as the baby grew inside her, she felt herself beginning to understand *why* it was that she had to endure it. Winn was away protecting the village from an army full of strange-looking men called the Mythria. She could sense him. Some days it was stronger than others. She had come to understand so much more of what her mother had taught her and even those lessons from Sekhet and the knowledge that the forest had given her. The wonder of the life growing within her filled her with a greater purpose for her life. She woke each morning from that awful day not with a dread but with a joy. Anwen felt as though she knew a great secret. The knowledge of which filled her with such joy that there was nothing else that could possibly dampen her spirit.

Winn had been gone almost four months, and often the news that came back to the village was not good. She heard of barbaric acts of the cruellest warfare. She often sat and thought about how blessed she was that she had not been born a male child, having to go off to war to defend your homeland and those that you love. War was such an unnatural act to Anwen. Knowing that all living things are linked she could never understand why it was that people could not just live in peace. There certainly was enough on this beautiful Earth to go and around. 'Owning' a piece of nature was not how she thought it was meant to be.

As was the daily ritual Anwen had taken herself down to the river to bathe. The cool water swirling around her feet always made her feel happy. The forest had such a healing effect, the dappled light reflecting of the water. As Anwen bent down to wash her face the baby moved and Anwen bolted upright, holding her belly to feel the movement. As she sat there holding her belly she could picture Winn. She saw him riding through a dense forest. This forest was not one she was familiar with, but she knew it to be in the lands not too far from home. Her heart filled with love as she could sense Winn on his horse. She felt that he was homeward bound and she turned to make her way home to prepare herself for his impending visit.

As she was making her way back to the house Anwen froze in her tracks, for out of the picture in her mind came another horse. Its rider was foreign to her. A man strangely attired. Her heart was racing as she saw Winn turn and spot his pursuer. Anwen ran back to the house calling Teleri to come quickly.

When she reached the house she was out of breath and it took her a moment to be able to calm herself to tell her grandmother what she had just experienced.

Teleri knew exactly what to do. She went into house and asked Anwen for the lock of hair that Winn had left behind with her. She took a piece from it and placed it in a piece of leaf from an elm tree. She added two or three other ingredients and tied the leaf shut. Teleri took the parcel and threw it into the fire, saying a prayer of protection over Winn.

Anwen spent the next two days in a state of agitation. She was not able to settle down, and being alone made her even more anxious, so she decided that the only way to get through the day would be to make herself useful.

CHAPTER SEVENTEEN

MARY

She made her way up to the kitchens of Ragland Castle. There Mary worked in the herb gardens and always appreciated help picking the herbs and sorting them. Mary often called on Anwen to discuss with her which herbs she thought would most likely go together in order to enhance the food of the Blathaon household. Mary knew the cook was always called before the lord to compliment her on this delicious food.

Anwen arrived at the castle and did what she always did when visiting—she stopped to just stand and look at it. She thought it was the most beautiful building she had ever seen. Apart from the fact that she had never seen any other building besides this one and so had no form of reference to compare it with she just knew that whatever was out there in the world could not compare with the beauty of Raglands which was alive with activity. There was news that Winn and his men were close to home and Lord Blathaon wanted a feast prepared in his honour. Anwen knew that there would be much to do within the kitchens and her help would be greatly appreciated.

Mary, a large woman with curly brown hair, greeted her with open arms. Her bosom seemed to rest on her belly and her belly reached her knees. It always made Anwen laugh when she saw her with her apron tied around her waist. So much cloth had been used to make the Apron that she was quite sure that it would make the most splendid table cloth for the great table in the Great Hall. Mary always smelled of pig fat and her little round blue eyes always had a sparkle to them, like she knew a very special secret.

The kitchen was small but light and warm and often there was not enough room for more than four people at any one time. Mary was so pleased to see Anwen and put her straight to work. The first thing she had her do was grind wheat to make the loaves of unleavened bread. Since Mary had to prepare a meal for at least fifty people, enough bread had to be baked.

The fire was red hot, and poor Thomas, who was Mary's son and thirteen years old, had been given the task of making sure the fire was always a certain temperature. He was also given the task of loading in the dough and making sure that the bread was taken out just as the crust turned a nice golden brown. He often got his ear bashed because Thomas was easily distracted and sometimes forgot something in the fire. The smell of the bread baking with the herbs she picked filled Anwen with a great joy. It was truly a blessing to be able to smell something so incredibly delicious.

Mary called in the hunters and gave them a list of animals that would be required to prepare the meal. A boar, some pheasant, deer, and fish was requested. It had to be a young boar and deer though. Mary did not want the meat to be tough.

There was a great commotion in the village when the soldiers, led by Winn, came home. Grandmothers, mothers, wives, lovers, brothers, and sisters lined the streets, all waving and shouting looking eagerly for their beloved. The men were weary and the horses were thin. The ravages of war were painted on their faces like masks. Broken and bruised they balanced on their trusted steeds.

As Anwen looked at them she noticed each carrying his own demons of war, eyes empty and void of life but sparking to life as each man caught a glimpse of a loved one. Anwen knew that some of these men would be forever altered; she hoped Winn would not be one of them. As she caught his eye she was distressed to see that his leg had been bandaged, but otherwise he looked strong and his eyes told her that he had made it through the other side without losing his soul. She knew he would because she had spent each day in the forest performing the ritual Teleri had shown her. She had cloaked him in a veil of strength. The men made their way to Ragland Castle, where they would dismount and go back home to rest.

As Winn came up alongside her he beckoned her to follow them up to the castle. He told her that he wished her to be at the dinner that was to be held and wanted her to be seated at his table in the great hall. Anwen dutifully followed, carried forward by the human wave of happiness and sadness . . . . Winn was delighted to note that Anwen was well and healthy.

As an expecting mother she looked more beautiful than he had ever seen her. One would barely know she was with child, but her stomach pushed out ever so slightly from beneath her skirts. Her breasts were full and round and her cheeks were pink, her jet black hair almost luminous it was so shiny. His heart swelled when he looked at this woman who had made something beautiful from something so vile. He could not wait to hear what she had been doing whilst he was away.

As he looked out on the crowd he saw the faces of those who would soon discover the fate of their loved ones and he felt sickened. The men who had died at his side had fought bravely and in the end lost, leaving behind a family that relied on the dead soldiers for their well-being. Winn knew that his father would not let these families starve, but there was only a certain amount of people they could help. The Mythrian army had arrived on their shores with a purpose to conquer and control and Winn had witnessed their incredible strength and resolve. He could not wait to tell Anwen of these strange and yet fascinating people. He had seen that they came from a culture that was advanced and educated and that they had moved across the continent like a swarm of locusts.

The war with them was not over and it lay heavy on his heart that he and his men had barely made a dent in their attack. He knew that it would be a matter of weeks before they would be on the outskirts of the untamed forest and in the villages. If not for the fact that Ragland was so well concealed because of the denseness of the forest it would probably have ended even sooner.

They still had so much to achieve, and he was not really sure how it would be that they would be able to survive. They Mythrian army planned to own this land he loved and make their women bear the Mythrian children, obliterating the Welsh and everything they had for centuries built. He needed to discuss this with Anwen, for he knew that she hailed from a family that had a great gift, and if they were going to protect this village it would take everyone and everything they knew to do so. Anwen believed in the ways of old and wished more people would embrace that and the laws of nature and the creatures within.

Winn made his way to his chambers where his father was waiting to greet him. With tears in his eyes he encouraged him to wash and prepare himself for the meal that had been prepared. They had much to discuss, but tonight would be a time of celebration and joy.

Winn told Anwen that he wanted to show her who it was they were fighting. Anwen would take him to the special tree, where she would make a fire and burn the leaves of the cipbar bush. Winn wouldn't have to do much but hold her hand and remember what he had seen. Anwen had the gift of sight and would be able to see everything as if she had been there herself.

CHAPTER EIGHTEEN

The Mythrian Army

The next day she waited patiently for Winn to arrive. It had been so good to see him the night before. She counted her blessings. It was indeed a blessing to be able to be present in the same space as the one you loved. As promised to her by the forest Anwen's desire for Winn had been totally satiated. Her love for him, however, would never assuage and it gave her the strength and wisdom to be who she was—a woman whose cachet was growing amongst her fellow villagers. In fact, after the news of her attack and Anwen's decision to keep the baby had been made public, the villagers tended to be more accepting of her and her methods and beliefs. Some had even ventured into the untamed forest for her counsel. The pity they felt towards this mysterious woman grew to admiration and, dare it be known, even adoration.

Anwen heard Winn coming, and she moved out into the dappled sunlight to greet him. She would take the time to look at his wound. He was limping, and she could tell that he was in some great discomfort. He had assured her that the wound was nothing.

He had taken a sword to the muscle in the top of his leg, and he indicated that the muscle had torn away from the bone. It had been difficult to keep clean, but Winn had tried his best. He had even made an effort to pack it with herbs that Anwen had given him. She had taught him where to find the sap of a certain plant that would seal the wound and allow it to heal. Unfortunately, Winn could not find this particular plant, and as a result the wound was constantly oozing.

He dismounted and tied his horse close by the edge of the river. As he moved towards Anwen he caught her scent and he scooped her up into his arms and held her close, holding her long enough for their souls to connect. They made their way inside the hollow tree, and Winn was amazed at how peaceful this place was, how incredibly concealed even though it was there quite obviously out in the open for all to see. He wondered if perhaps there was a magic spell that concealed its entrance and only those privileged few would know of its existence.

The interior of the tree shined, another thing Winn could not understand. It looked like he was beneath a clear night sky, the stars flashing on and off like the fireflies across a plain.

They seated themselves and made themselves comfortable. Anwen prepared the leaves and began the ritual, all the while making chitchat. Winn was totally at ease and began to recount the tales of the Mythrian army. Anwen took his hands and closed her eyes.

Anwen could smell them before she saw them. A mixture of sweat and something that smelt like burnt honey. She 'watched' Winn carefully move up a small hill hiding behind trees and shrubs. The Mythrian army had set up camp in a valley below and the man on watch was asleep against a tree. As Winn glanced down upon the men the air was sucked from Anwen's lungs. Never before had she 'seen' assembled so many men in such a small space. She could not count them all, but if she had to hazard a guess she imagined that perhaps there were at least four hundred. Some wore red tunics while others wore what looked to her like a very short dress, white in colour.

The men guarding the main shelter were in full uniform in red tunics with bronze body armour, shiny and bright and very formidable looking. Worn upon their heads were helmets adorned with a red plume. She could not believe the extent of their weaponry, banners, and flags. They looked like a nest of red and bronzed termites busily going about their duties with purpose. Just looking at them she realised that these people were well advanced. She could smell the wood fires and the horses grazing peacefully on the outskirts of the camp.

In the middle of the camp was a very large structure made from a red and white fabric. It was heavily guarded and Anwen presumed that this was where the leader of this army resided. All the men were thickly set, and as Anwen was drawn to a battle that Winn's men had encountered against this great army, it appeared to Anwen that the Mythrian army was graded into five classes, and from these classes, in varying degrees, were recruited the ranks of the army. The most wealthy, the first class, were the most heavily armed, equipped with helmets, round shields, greaves, and breastplates, all of bronze, and carrying spears and swords. The lesser classes bore lesser armament and weaponry, a group of them carrying no armour at all, solely armed with slings. Those men who rode the horses had been trained in the art of warfare upon a horse and this was their charge.

Anwen saw that as they planned their attack they arranged themselves into three lines of soldiers. At the front stood the spearmen. In the second row stood the young fighters who carried body armour and a rectangular shield. As weapons they carried a sword and javelins. Standing next to these fighters were far more lightly armed men, carrying only a spear.

Then the men of experience and maturity had the younger and inexperienced men stand beside them to draw the attention of Winn's men. They were dressed in fancy regalia and gave the impression that they were the experienced soldiers. A total ruse, for in fact whilst they were busy creating a diversion, it was then that the experienced men were able to lay a fatal blow to the unsuspecting opponent.

This was how Winn had been injured. He had taken on one of these men and had been attacked from the side. He surely would have perished if it had not been for Folant, who had never left his master's side and watched as this mountain of a man thrust forward with his sword aiming for Winn's midriff. Folant threw himself forward at this man, setting him off balance, and his blow went askew. Winn had easily taken the life of the soldier and turned to face the man who had driven a sword through his leg. Had Winn not been so quick-witted he would not have reached Folant in time, but Winn threw his spear and hit Folant's assailant at the base of his skull, severing his spinal cord, instantly rendering him incapacitated.

There was a group of men wielding slingshots, hurling small rocks into the thick of Winn's army. Anwen 'watched' with growing trepidation as she saw the horsemen moving into attack. These were the soldiers of importance and breeding, and she watched as Winn instructed his men to fall back and retreat, realising that they were no match for this adversary.

She sat there gathering her thoughts. She slowed her breathing and cast her mind's eye over the valley towards the sea. She felt broken and could picture the light of her soul like fireflies scattered over the earth. She needed to centre herself and put all the pieces back together so she could find the strength to take on one of the hardest tasks she had been given. So many people relied upon her at this moment. She needed to be able to find the intention of this army and whether her village would still be at risk. She knew she was required to help avert this tragedy, the annihilation of her people. She knew she would need to cast her mind into the midst of the army generals. Anwen needed to create an illusion filled with superstition and mysticism that would cause the logic and known understanding of man to be abandoned, causing them to flee and forget their purpose. Did she have this power to wield? She did, for she knew of such mysticism and knew of the power of the mind. She knew that anything born from a thought could be manifested physically.

She smiled across at Winn and said, 'They have fled and are not returning!'

CHAPTER NINETEEN

After the meeting with Anwen in the great tree, Winn felt as though life would, after all, shine kindly on him as he readied himself for the day. He knew that this was the day he knew they needed to talk about what the future held for them. He longed for her to be his wife.

As Winn made his way to Teleri's dwelling he recalled the conversation that he had had with his father, Lord Blathaon, the night before. By the time he had reached home after hearing what Anwen had believed to be 'truth', as far as the Mythrian army was concerned he was agitated, but only because it was the recollection of that time in his life, which reeked on the garment of his memory and he could not settle to anything.

His father heard his son pacing in the great hall. Lord Blathaon found Winn standing in front of one of the great fireplaces in the great hall. Just the one was stoked, and Winn was busy putting logs on the fire.

As Winn picked up his goblet of mead Lord Blathaon noted that his son's hand was shaking uncontrollably. The past few months had been difficult ones. Firstly the dreadful death of that girl from the village and the impending threat of war with the Mythrian's hung heavy on his heart. As ruler of this land it was Blathaon's duty to protect his people, and he knew that he had the love and respect of his domain. He was disturbed to note that Winn had been distracted of late and he could no longer wait for him to come to him and tell him what it was that was distressing him so.

Winn looked up and saw his father coming down the stairwell. The beautiful bannister of the stairwell crafted so lovingly by Anwen's father. It seemed that whichever way he turned she was there in some form or another. He could not believe that the gentle man who had crafted this magnificent banister was also deceased, along with his incredible sons. Winn's heart ached, for he could not believe that his beloved could have endured so much heartache and so much loss and yet still continued to smile and seemed to always have a song in her heart.

Winn had spent many wonderful times with Anwen's brothers even before he had met her on the Day of Festivals. They had been specially requested by Lord Blathaon. Aneirin, Anwen's older brother, and he had spent many hours practising their jousting and swordsman skills. Although Aneirin was a commoner, Winn had been told of his strength and talent in this field and had respected his ability to enable Winn to sharpen his tactics. Cass and Gareth, his younger brothers, had always come along to watch and sat eager to be allowed the chance to participate. Winn smiled remembering a wrestling match they had all had once. He'd had found a camaraderie amongst the brothers that he lacked in his own family. Winn had not had the chance to fully know his siblings.

Winn greeted his father with a hug and poured him some mead. He walked back over to the fireplace where he stood for a moment longer before he would have to speak of the thing that was troubling his heart; he sensed that

that was why he had come to see him. How was he going to tell his father that the woman he loved was a commoner who had been defiled and carried the child of her rapist, yet he still wanted to have her for his own? His mind juggled with the realisation that even as he thought it, he could understand that it was so totally absurd.

How was he going to tell his father that he had avenged Anwen and taken another man's life? His heart sank as he realised that this perhaps would be the one and only time in his life that he would have disappointed his father. He steeled himself and faced his father head on. The words seemed to come out in a gush and it appeared as if he didn't even stop to breathe. He told him of how he had met Anwen, of the days he had spent getting to know her. Lord Blathaon had known her father and brothers, and so knew something of their family.

Winn told his father how he had found her in the forest and what had been done to her. Lord Blathaon moved to the fire and threw his mead into the flames. He started pacing as he realised where his son was going with his tale. Winn continued telling his father how incredibly strong Anwen was and that she had no intention of ridding herself of the baby within her belly. That, in fact, she had remarkably embraced the child as a blessing from nature.

Lord Blathaon frowned and shook his head. He would not understand this; he could not, for he did not understand. Winn then explained that on that day he had found Anwen he had later tracked Cedrick and his brothers and was sure that indeed it was they who had done this terrible thing. He tried to explain that he was torn in two and was consumed with anger. He then told his father that he had found Cedrick and confronted and killed him.

Lord Blathaon exhaled for what seemed like eternity. The air in the room was crisp and cold in spite of the roaring fire. Winn thought that his father would shatter like a shard of ice. Winn continued telling his father that he loved Anwen with all his heart and soul and that he did not care about his heritage. All he wanted was for her to be his wife if she would have him.

Lord Blathaon moved over to his son and held him at arm's length. He then said something that Winn had not expected. He had told him to follow his heart—that he had noted that Winn was in love and in his eyes there was nothing more wonderful to be able to find the love of your life. He did not know how it would all come to pass but that he had his support.

Winn had felt as though the weight of the world had been lifted from his shoulders. He had been given his father's blessing and validation that what he had done was honourable. Morvudd, the woman who had been selected for Winn was a noble lady from another county and he knew that she would have made Winn a good wife, and since she was fair of face he had no doubt that Winn would have learned to love her. But with Anwen as his interest Morvudd was no competition. He could not expect his son to live out his existence, half existing.

Winn had left his father that night and retired to his chambers, and he slept soundly for the first time in many months.

CHAPTER TWENTY

Where life, all life, reached its esoteric comprehension

He had the whole day planned. He was going to take Anwen to the river to the spot by the tree—her tree—the sacred place that only he and her family had known existed. He had asked Mary to pack a picnic lunch of only the best foods, filled with things he knew Anwen loved. He was going to ask her to be his wife. His palms were sweaty and the back of his throat itched. Never before had he been so nervous.

When he got to the cottage Anwen was standing waiting outside for him. She was in a dress that had been stained a very pale pink colour. He suspected that it was from one of the many flowers she grew. It was as though her frock was blushing, for the colour was not constant throughout. She had made a hair tie in the same fabric and had woven a very small rose into the side of her hair. Her cheeks were slightly pink and her lips were a deep red. Her brown eyes seemed to glow, and again Winn was struck by the sense that he felt as though he would 'fall into her' and never return. When she saw him her face transformed into a radiant smile and he knew at that moment that there would never be another moment in his life when he would know with all certainty that he was loved. Loved beyond this life and loved in a way that transcended all human comprehension.

He did not understand how it was that when he was around Anwen, he felt complete. He pulled up next to her and dismounted. He took the small basket she had prepared and tied it next to the one he'd had Mary prepare. He was tempted to tell her to leave hers behind, but he knew that she would have something special in her basket and without it their day would not be the same. After he had secured the baskets in place he moved over to her and embraced her. Her smell was intoxicating, and the warmth of her body made him feel dizzy. He wasn't really sure how he was going to lift her onto his horse without dropping her. He was especially aware of not doing that since she was with child and knew how important this baby was to Anwen despite how it came to be. He thought at that moment that he would never again know such a strong and compassionate person.

Anwen suggested that he mount his steed first and then reached down to pull her up behind him. Winn agreed and when he bent down to lift her she slid behind him without any difficulty. Anwen was very good handling a horse. Her brothers had taught her lots of tricks and how to ride with conviction. She straightened her dress and made herself comfortable behind him and slipped her hands around his chest, pressing her body up against his back.

She could feel his heart beating and was pleased to note that it was in time with the beating of her heart. She smiled and said, 'Ready when you are!'

She told Winn that they would not be going to the tree but somewhere even more special, a place she had not been to in a very long time. The last time she had been there was with her mother when she was a little girl and she was not even sure she would be able to find it. They headed off in the same direction and after riding for some time Winn saw up ahead a great thickness in the already thick forest.

It became apparent that the forest was too thick to take his horse into, so they took all they needed and tethered him to a tree. Anwen laid down the basket she was carrying and turned to face him. She told him that from this moment on it was very important not to speak. If he needed to talk to her he was to whisper close to her ear. She explained that never again would he experience anything like this and it was only if he promised to do as she said would she allow them to continue forward.

Winn was intrigued, a little apprehensive, and quite afraid that he would not fulfil his obligation to her today, whatever that was to be.

As they moved forward into the thick of the trees it was as though the trees embraced them. All around the air was thick, a most wonderful mist. It was a light, warm mist. The light bounced off like it was raining glitter. The air was pungent with the most incredible smell, and Winn felt very lightheaded. He seemed to lose his sense of direction. He could see Anwen in front of him moving through the mist, and it seemed to caress her body—the contrast of her black hair in the glistening light in the blanket of green that enveloped them.

Winn was aware that there was no sound other than his heart pounding in his ears. He could not even hear his feet as he moved over the undergrowth, a mixture of moss and ferns. It smelt like honey and mint and wet dirt, with a hint of something exotic.

Anwen reached back and took his hand and drew him closer to her side. Slowly she moved towards what seemed like an opening in the thick of the green shade. He could see a faint glow up ahead and was aware that that would be the point at which they would stop.

They stepped through the mist into an area no bigger than perhaps four very large blankets set next to one another. The air was still warm but very clean and somehow very bright although they were surrounded by massive trees. Creepers and flowers cascaded down from these big trees, the colours of which he had never before seen. This was the source of the aroma he'd smelled.

The flowers almost seemed iridescent, and he suspected that this was where Anwen had gotten the flowers to make that potion he had seen in her room that night he had taken her out of the forest after Cedrick had raped her. He could not take his eyes off them. The harder he looked the more he saw. He let go of Anwen's hand and gestured to her that he could not believe what he was looking at. She smiled and touched his lips to remain quiet. She opened her basket and then laid out the blankets he had brought. She took out a loaf of bread and a vial with an orange liquid in it. They sat on the blanket and ate what he had brought. With neither of them speaking their senses were heightened and the food seemed to taste even more delicious.

Once they'd had their fill Anwen took two crudely crafted wooden goblets from her basket and poured a small amount of the liquid in each. She moved close to Winn and told him that she wanted him to drink. The smell of her breath on his face was almost too much for him to bear. He was suffocating in the pain it caused him not to reach out and crush her to him. He took the wooden goblet and drank the liquid. It was incredibly sweet and left a very bitter aftertaste in his mouth. Anwen drank hers and then beckoned for him to lie beside her on the blanket.

As he laid his head next to hers, holding her hand, he closed his eyes. What happened next he would never in all his life be able to understand or disclose.

Winn felt as though he was somehow lifting off the ground but was indeed standing. Anwen stood next to him. He was startled to note that although this was the case, 'he' was still lying next to 'her' on the blanket. Anwen understood he was afraid of this realisation, and she touched his cheek to reassure him. Her touch was warm and soothing.

Anwen reached down and took his hand, and holding his gaze, she said, "Today is the day I will give myself to you. I can never marry you and be your wife. I cannot be whole in the world we live in, and I love you too much to destroy what you have prepared yourself for. This will be the only time I will be with you but it will be enough. We will never want for each other again in this world. I was told that this time would be given to me, and it is now. The love that will transcend from this moment will quench our desire and will carry us to the next. I know that one day we will find each other in another "time" because of this moment and we will have the chance to spend a lifetime together growing old and watching our children and grandchildren. The baby growing in my belly will one day show you why it is that we cannot be together and why it has to happen this way. I don't even know the reason. All I know is that I have to love this child and protect her. I have been given this chance to be with you, but I have to promise it will never happen again'.

She said that although it would appear real to them both, in reality it would not have physically happened.

Winn was crushed and confused and wanted to run, but his feet could not move. There were a thousand things swirling around in his head, and he had so many things to say, so many objections, yet she reached up and put her fingers to his lips. She drew him to her and whispered in his ear, 'Hold me close, for this is when our souls will embrace'. Then she stepped back from him and started to undress herself.

He did not want to go any longer, and he watched as she untied the front of her pale pink gown. It fell to the ground, and he was shocked that she was completely naked. She was the most beautiful creature he had ever seen. Her shoulders were soft and white and her hair hung down over her breasts. Her nipples were a pale pink. Her belly was perfect and her legs were long and strong and wonderful. He noted that she had a distinctive mole over the bottom of her right rib cage. It was in the shape of a butterfly.

She stepped forward and undressed him and pressed up against his body. She put his hands on her hips and pressed her mouth to his. Her mouth was warm and sweet. She kissed him for a long time, and it was as though time had stopped. Winn was reminded of the embrace they had that night he had been with Teleri and Anwen and had spoken of his encounter with Cedrick. It was not just an embrace; it was a spiritual experience that came from a place deep within their souls.

At this point he could not help himself. He lifted her and gently lay her down. From here Winn took the time to look at her. He explored every inch of her body, drinking in her form into his mind. The hair on her navel and hip bone glistened white in contrast to the deep black of the hair between her legs. Winn kissed every part of her and then parted her lips and kissed her with a deep desire. She responded to him, moaning softly and whispering that she loved him with all her soul. Anwen then looked at Winn, this beautiful man, and her heart pounded with centuries of longing. She felt the blood in her veins and it felt like fire. He was the most beautiful man she had ever seen and would ever see again in her life. The muscles in his body were defined, and although he was a big man she noted that he was not a rough man. His skin was soft to the touch, and under her fingers it felt like velvet. The smell of his body was intoxicating and she felt as though she actually wanted to 'eat' him. She kissed his body and moved her tongue over his skin, tasting him and storing him in the memory banks of her mind. His blue eyes were such a contrast against his black eyelashes, and he seemed to look straight into her soul.

Anwen gave into the moment and her spirit soared as Winn moved on top of her, and as he entered that warm and sacred place she held him close and together they discovered the wonder of love. As she reached her climax Winn noticed that Anwen stopped breathing, and in an explosion of joy she held him even tighter. He could taste her tears and feel her trembling beneath him. She cried deep racking sobs and he joined her in the moment. The tears were for joy. For what seemed a very long time they stayed coupled together, too afraid to move and destroy the moment—that one moment when their souls were joined in something so pure.

They stayed in that place throughout the night and explored each other until the sun began to rise and Winn was conscious that he could feel the numbness in his legs and arms. He realised that he was once again lying on the blanket next to his beloved Anwen. He turned to look at her and she was crying. The light from the morning sun was not strong, but it gave enough light to once again be able to see the beautiful cascade of flowers. Winn was convinced that during the night someone had come and changed the flowers, for they were a completely different colour and the combination of colours had changed. He stood up and walked over to them. He reached out to pick a very blue flower, and as his hand touched the bloom it changed to a deep red colour. Anwen stood up and moved over to his side. She told him that this was a very rare flower that took on the colour of the person's mood.

The colours that they were witnessing were the colours reflected off Winn and Anwen. She told him that he could not just pick these blooms there was a process to being able to harvest them and only Teleri knew how it was done. She had never been told how. She suggested that perhaps it would be best to leave them be. She turned him to face her and jumped up into his arms. Winn caught her and held her turning circles till he became dizzy and they both fell down. They laughed until they cried and then she told him that it was time to leave. They would go to the river and bathe together and then make their way back.

As they left the tree Winn turned to look at the place one last time and was shocked to see that it was no longer, that instead it was now dense and dark. Anwen took his hand and kept making her way out towards the light. They spotted his horse peacefully grazing, still tethered to the tree.

Winn tied everything back onto the horse's back and they made their way down to the river. It was a beautiful morning. The sky was blue and the air was fresh and clean. As they came to the spot by the tree Anwen undressed and slipped into the water. It was cold and she gasped as she dived under the crystal clear water. Winn watched her for a moment. He wanted to remember this moment, for he knew that never again would he see her do this. She swam and glided under the water as if she were a water creature.

At one point she held her breath and dived to the bottom of the river, where she then turned over onto her back. He could see her looking up through the water at the sky. She lay perfectly still. The light was rippling off her white body. Her hair was moving to and fro like a mass of seaweed. She looked like a mythical creature, a water sprite. She smiled up at him and beckoned him to come in.

Winn took off his clothes and slipped into the water so as not to stir it up too much and swam on top of her, gathering her to him. She was warm in contrast to the cold of the water and they held on to each other till they could no longer hold their breath. This was the first time they had physically held each other and yet it did not feel the same as it had the night before. It was not as intense, and it was at this point that Winn began to believe that what Anwen had told him was true, that the time they had shared would complete them and fill their desires for each other. Although they knew that never again would they love another as they had, it was stored in their hearts and from this moment on they would be happy and content just to be able to be around one another for as long as this life would allow.

They finished swimming and then Anwen told him that they needed to get back to the cottage where she would be able to finish telling him her thoughts.

Winn was not sure that he would be able to accept what she had told him the night before, yet as he rode back to the cottage he was completely at peace. He knew that he could not question what she had told him. He did not want to. He knew that Anwen had to continue on to have the baby and that she would be okay. He knew that the journey destiny was taking him on did not include her, and for the first time since he'd met her, he was not distressed. Quite the opposite—he was happy. The memory of the last twenty-four hours moved through his body, coating it in thick, delicious ecstasy. He knew that this would be something that would never leave him. Life may try to wear it thin but he was sure that even if he lived to be very old, he would go to his grave with the essence of Anwen's love surrounding him. He could not explain why or what had happened to make him have this change of heart, and he wasn't sure that he would be able to explain it to his father, especially since he had just spent the night telling his father that he would give up everything for Anwen.

He smiled at the wonder of the woman he'd had the privilege of loving. He was excited that he would still be able to engage in her life and knew there would still be much he would learn from her and gain from being in her company.

He laughed out loud and kicked his horse to gallop home. Anwen held on tighter and was laughing so hard he feared she may lose her grip and fall off. He loved the way she laughed. Although she was small her laughter was loud and deep and seemed to come right from the pit of her stomach. Oh how blessed he felt and how totally in tune with nature and the world.

CHAPTER TWENTY-ONE

Anwen called for Rhona to push harder. She could see the baby's head crowning. She was soaked with sweat, and after twelve hours in labour she was weak and tired. Anwen had been called in the middle of the night to help Rhona give birth. Rhona was only eighteen years old, and this baby had been conceived out of wedlock. Rhona had come to see Anwen when she was in her fourth month. She was afraid and alone, for the man who had helped get her into this state had gone off to fight against the Mythrian army, and he had been one of the first of their village who had been killed.

Rhona had been lost in the deep catacombs of depression and did not know which way to turn. She knew that she would be ostracised by the villagers and branded a harlot, but she and Sion had planned to marry when he returned. It was not to be, and when Rhona had missed her second moon she knew that she was with child. She loved Sion and had no intention of 'doing away' with the baby. She, like Anwen, understood the importance of life. She was going to have this baby in spite of what it would mean for her.

Anwen had spent the next few months tending to her needs, administering various herbs and medicines to help her with her morning sickness, and making sure she kept strong and healthy.

When Anwen had left in the middle of the night the sky was alight with a pending storm—the likes of which Anwen was sure she had never known. The wind was strong and it took her even longer to reach Rhona because as fast as she moved forward, the force of the wind pushed her back. Anwen was now almost nine months pregnant and although she was strong and healthy she was finding it more difficult to do the things she normally did with ease. The bag she was carrying with the things she would need made it even more cumbersome for her.

Rhona's little brother, Taren, had run his heart out and arrived breathless and in a state. He had been sent to call her to please come and help. He was afraid of the storm that was coming, and no sooner had he relayed the message, he turned and darted off back into the blackness.

She left soon after that, once she had gotten her things together. Teleri already had a special bag packed for birthing mothers. Anwen simply added a few extra things (those things that she had come to learn, those things that she was now able to show her grandmother). She smiled as she packed them into the bag.

Remembering her mother, she knew that Branwenn would have been so proud of how much she had learnt and how she had taken special care to listen to those words that were not directly spoken, those words that came from the heart of people—the 'true person'—and from nature itself.

Anwen moved faster, and as she came to cross over the river the trees were swaying to and fro, creaking and groaning and straining against the force of the wind. The bridge that her brother Aneirin had built was swaying to and fro, and she wondered if she would make it across without being thrown off and tossed into the river and swept away. The bridge itself was very strong but the water was moving very quickly and the sound it was making was no longer a gentle trickling sound—it was now a thunderous roar over the rocks.

Anwen kissed the talisman around her neck and stepped onto the bridge. Strangely, she did not feel she was in danger, for she knew that the river would certainly not be the place where she would meet her demise. If anything she was quite sure that if she did fall in that the swirls of water would carry her safely to the bank. She was still nevertheless afraid for her baby and said a prayer to Mother Nature to help her cross safely. The wind was blowing her hair and was whipping it across her face and stinging her eyes, causing them to fill with tears.

She continued forward, knowing that the little momentum she had was keeping her from falling over. The darkness above her was threatening to pluck her up and swallow her. There were great clashes of thunder, and the lightening was so bright it lit up the ground like it was day, giving her some reprieve and helping to ensure that she was not walking into a deep hole or into another equally nasty place.

As soon as it grew dark there was another bolt of lightning and it was so close together, the sequencing of these natural phenomena, that she was almost able to make her whole way there without stumbling.

Rhona was a slight girl, and Anwen feared that the birth would not go smoothly. Rhona grew weary and was starting to panic that things were not running smoothly. Outside, the storm was raging. The sky was ablaze with all the fury of nature. Being a superstitious person, Rhona feared the worst. She had only known Anwen a few short months and had not yet come to understand that though Anwen was young she was wise far beyond her years. She had not come to learn that Anwen had the blessing of all that is good and anything she was tasked to do would almost always turn out for the best.

Anwen reached into her bag and took out that vial of orange liquid. She placed one drop onto Rhona's tongue. It only took a minute for the effect to take hold. Immediately she relaxed.

As she lay there, the sounds around her changed from a frightening tornado to the most incredible orchestra of music. She could hear the instruments of nature playing a tune of rebirth. The pain she was feeling was somehow absorbed into the air around her, and she was suddenly aware of what it was that she was doing. She was giving birth to a life, something that had been done for centuries, and now it was her turn.

How she performed this would be forever burned in her memory. Rhona took a deep breath, and she could smell Anwen, that familiar smell of honey and earth and cooked potatoes and she knew she had nothing to fear. As the baby moved from her body out into the great body of the world, Rhona cried tears of joy. Anwen took the precious child and laid him in her arms. He was perfect except for a birth mark at the base of his spine. Rhona tenderly touched it and told Anwen in a matter of fact way that this was how Sion had died—he'd had a spear pierce the base of his spine. It was in that moment that she realised she had made the right choice in allowing the baby to live.

Anwen delivered the afterbirth and took the time to help Rhona clean herself and burn the bloodied pieces of cloth. Anwen did not realise how important this child would be. Rhona kissed him and said in the traditional way, 'Welcome, my darling child. You shall be called Loan, which means "God's gift".'

As the storm raged on, Anwen sat with Rhona and her new baby, watching them discovering each other. She was growing anxious, for it was now many hours since she had left Teleri and was afraid that she may now be wondering what had happened to her. Anwen knew her grandmother and knew that in spite of what was happening around her she would head out in search of her granddaughter. Anwen's heart was gripped in panic at the thought of Teleri trying to make her way over the bridge. The rules that applied to Anwen did not apply to Teleri, and she knew that the full vengeance of the storm would be unleashed upon her grandmother should she fall into the river.

Anwen stood up and started to pack her things together. She told Rhona that she had to go home now. No amount of persuasion could change her mind, and she headed out into the storm. Although it was now light the sky was still very dark—in fact, it was the most unusual light Anwen had ever seen. It was not light as daylight should be, it was more of a glow. The glow was not white though but more of a yellow-pink colour. It was bright enough for her to see the ravages of the wind. All manner of leaves and branches were strewn around.

As Anwen got closer to the river she also noticed the debris of a roof scattered like litter in the market square. She recognised this to be the roof from her grandmother's house. Anwen's heart raced, and she began to run. The length of her petticoats and the weight of the bag she was carrying slowed her down to barely a trot, and Anwen had to place her hand beneath her belly to enable herself to move quicker. The ground was wet and muddy and very dangerous to traverse and with each step she took she said a prayer that she would not fall.

She made it to the banks of the river and was about to cross when she noticed her grandmother's shawl caught in the reeds a short way down the river. Anwen's heart sank and she froze. She could feel the bile rising in her stomach and had to pinch herself to control the emotion that was pumping through her body.

Anwen stepped onto the bridge and moved slowly to the other side, for the logs were wet and slippery. She put the bag down by the special tree and made her way carefully through the debris alongside of the banks of the river. The emotion of what she was feeling brought to mind the last time she'd experienced this. It was not even during that day with Cedrick. It was the time she had returned to her family home to discover there was nothing left of anything she held dear. There was only the ashes of a once beautiful dwelling and the charred remains of her father and mother and darling brothers, the memory of which she would never be able to erase.

Lying in the grips of their deathly pose was her mother's body holding Gareth. Her father was holding Cass, and in turn Aneirin was seated behind both his parents with his arms around them. They'd had to break the bodies to pull them apart to bury the remains, and Anwen knew that to the very end, love was the only thing they felt. Not the pain of the fire, not fear of their impending death, only love.

With this memory Anwen realised that she had tears rolling down her cheeks and perspiration on her brow. She was praying now to Mother Nature to please spare her the pain of having to lose the only living relative left to her.

She made her way to the same spot where Cedrick had pushed Braith into the water that day, to the place where she had had to pull his lifeless body out of the water. There was a bend in the river at this spot and the reeds formed a natural net, catching all that washed down in its claws.

There in the catchment lay the cold and lifeless body of her darling Teleri. Her petticoats were wrapped around her body like an ancient funeral dressing. Her hair was tangled in the vines, which were holding her in place. Teleri's eyes were open and her mouth was agape, like a fish caught on a hook. The life drained from its eyes as it is pulled from the depths of its paradise. Anwen could not contain her anguish. She fell to her knees at the side of the river in the yellow-pink light, in the swirl of the wind, and screeched out a wail.

She could not move from this position, and the only thing she was able to do was scream and cry till her throat was hoarse and dry. The tears streamed down her face, and her hair was wet and stuck to her like mud. She crawled forward and lowered herself gently into the water just behind the basket-like catchment area her grandmother was lying in.

The baby in her stomach gave her buoyancy, and she found it quite difficult to keep her feet on the river bed. She wedged her feet into the mud up to her knees and reached forward to slowly try and free her grandmother's hair from the branches. As she was working she was thinking about how she was going to then lift Teleri out of the river. The bank of the river was steep, and she didn't know how she was going to get herself out. Anger flooded Anwen and steeled her to continue with her task no matter how obviously hopeless it was going to be.

As she freed her grandmother and wrapped her arms around her lifeless body, Anwen popped up out of the riverbed, and the two of them were carried down the river.

The swirling water filled every orifice it could find, sucking her and her grandmother beneath its surface.

Anwen was suddenly aware that she was not alone. Beneath the murky waters she could see the form of another being, a familiar being. As the being moved closer to them she realised that it was Sekhet. She was smiling at Anwen and moved behind her and seemed to push her through the water. When Anwen looked up above the surface of the water she noticed that one of the roof trusses had wedged itself in the side of the river. They floated towards it, and as if they had no weight at all, they glided over and on top of the trestle. Anwen lay there coughing and gagging and trying to catch her breath. She could hardly breathe.

The baby in her belly was kicking violently and shifting from side to side. Anwen sat up and grasped her stomach and slowed down her breathing. She took long deep breaths, the oxygen filling her system and relaxing the muscles around the baby. After some minutes she managed to stand up, and after tying her hair in a knot she looked around to see where it was that she had landed.

To her dismay she had come so far down river that she was now in the place where the river moved through the hunting forest. This was the very place where Cedrick had chased her. She knew there was an opening in the forest not too far from where she was, and this was where Winn had found her. She had not been back to this part of the forest since that day and was not sure that she could move through that area to go and get someone to help her.

She tried to pull Teleri's body higher so that half of her lay on the trestle, the other half on the bank of the river. She kissed her grandmother's forehead and turned to make her way towards Ragland Castle. It would be a long walk and she was not sure she would make it. There was, however, no other alternative. Each step she took was like moving through a quagmire. The ground was wet and muddy, her clothes were wet and heavy, and her legs just would not move forward. She was growing tired and weak and the baby had stopped moving in her belly. She was so afraid that something was wrong.

CHAPTER TWENTY-TWO

Linn

The storm was dissipating but the wind was still blowing strong, and being wet she was now feeling extremely cold. This made it even more difficult for her to move forward. Her legs felt like they belonged to another, and although her heart was pumping, Anwen felt as though she was a walking corpse. She realised that with everything that had happened it would make it difficult for anyone to find her, and she decided that she should try to leave some kind of a trail in the direction she had taken just in case Winn came looking. She knew that he would, for every day since that special day they had spent together he had taken time from each day to make sure he spent time in her company. The bond between them was strong and pure and had grown into something that Anwen knew both she and Winn would never again in this life have with anyone else. Anwen knew that she had taught him enough about the forest to make it easy enough to realise she was leaving clues. She tore pieces of her petticoats and tied it to various branches of trees and bushes.

As she neared the spot where Cedrick had attacked her she began to grow faint. This was for two reasons: first, she had not eaten for many hours, and second, she was anxious. Anwen chastised herself, telling herself it was only a place, which, after all was in the forest she loved. The place she felt most at home.

Yet, as she came to the spot, panic rose within her. She could not take another step. Anchored to the spot she was forced to stand there and remember her attack. She could see the whole scene unravelling before her. There were ghosts of Cedrick and his brothers taunting and dancing around her broken body.

Anwen felt the blood drain from her head, and she had no way of stopping what was about to happen. She fell backwards, feeling her consciousness fading. She did not remember hitting the ground.

Anwen lay in the mud as the sun pushed its way through the clouds. She lay there for some hours, and by the time she regained consciousness it was early evening. Her body was stiff from the cold, and her feet and hands were blue. She started shivering and tried to get up. As she moved, a searing pain moved through her body and exploded in her belly. She felt a warm liquid between her legs and realised with horror that her water had broken. The labour pain was intense and draining and since she knew she did not have much strength, she feared that she would die out there in the middle of nowhere.

She crawled on her hands and knees between contractions and managed to move herself into the dense growth of the forest. The ground was soft but not muddy. It had all manner of ferns and moss. Anwen knew that she had to find a place that was a little dryer, out of the elements, and hidden from predators.

The forest was full of foxes and wild boar. Anwen was gripped in pain, and it was difficult to think straight. She called out a prayer of protection, she called out for Sekhet, and she called out for Teleri and her parents and brothers. There was, needless to say, no response, only the blackness, and its inky form seemed to move around her and suffocate the life from her veins.

Anwen passed out again and woke with her contractions tearing her apart. Some time must have passed for the dawn was nigh and she could see the faint glow of the sun above the tops of the trees within the forest. The pain was so severe she vomited, and choking on the bile and tears she lay there thinking that perhaps she had made the wrong choice in deciding to keep this baby.

This life had been conceived out of violence, not love. Alone she had endured the assault and alone she would be giving birth. She lay there and tried to concentrate to try and connect with Winn to call him to her. Anwen managed to move herself up against a pile of rocks covered in moss, and she prepared herself for something she had helped so many other women do.

She squatted with her legs spread as far apart as she could get them, supporting her body with her arms around her knees and pressing the small of her back up against the rocks. As she reached down between her legs she could feel the baby's head crowning.

The pain was coming almost every minute now, and she knew that at any moment now the baby would enter this world. Since she had fainted twice already this was what she was trying hard to avoid. As she looked up she noticed a little bush with a distinctly shaped leaf. She was angry that she had not noticed it before. She reached out and broke off a small twig. Her grandmother had taught her that if you chewed the bark of this bush it had a very bitter taste but it gave you strength.

The effect did not last long but it was enough, Anwen knew, to enable her to have the baby and deliver the afterbirth without fainting. As she chewed on the bark it was so bitter that she thought she would retch again. She managed to swallow the spittle in her mouth and almost immediately she felt energised and alive. The pain was incredible, and with all her effort she took a deep breath and bore down hard, pushing the baby from within.

Anwen caught the child before it hit the ground and looked with awe at the creature in her hands. She was perfect in every way. She was petit and elfin-like with the most incredible amount of deep auburn hair. In fact it was more black than red, or was it more red than black? Anwen could not decide, and the light was not strong enough for her to tell exactly. The baby cried, and Anwen tore the rest of her petticoats to wrap her in. The cloth was wet, and she knew that this was not a good thing so she worked quickly to sever the umbilical cord using a twig from the same branch to clamp the end of the cord on the baby. She laid the child down and with the last contraction delivered the afterbirth, pushing down on her belly from the outside and pulling the cord from between her legs. The afterbirth came away like moss off a rock, and after checking it was in once piece she dug a hole and buried it so as not to attract the animals in the forest. Next she fashioned a sling in which she placed the baby and tied it across her chest. This would generate enough warmth to keep the wind off the wet cloth and enable the baby to keep warm. Anwen then sat back against the rocks and looked down at the child, her big green eyes trying to focus in the darkness.

As Anwen lay there looking at her child, she realised that something was missing from around her neck.

With panic-stricken horror she realised the talisman that had been passed down to her from the generations of her family was no longer there. Anwen searched the area she was sitting in and ran to the spot where she had fainted, still nothing. Anwen was trembling and called out to her grandmother. It was at this point that she remembered why it was she had come to be in this place, and the memory filled her mind, sucking the life from her soul. Teleri was gone. Her darling grandmother had died without seeing her great-granddaughter.

Anwen fell to the ground consumed with grief. She felt as though she had been stripped of everything. The baby was making suckling noises and it was foreign and frightening and at that moment she wanted to dump the baby and run. She wanted to be alone and as far away from Raglands as possible. She wanted her mother and her father and her brothers. She wanted Winn, and she wanted life to be as it had been.

Anwen rocked back and forth as the baby was now crying and it was a maternal instinct to comfort the child. She felt detached and numb and had no idea how she would be able to look after this child without a home, without Teleri, and without the talisman that had kept her safe until this point. Anwen could not see the forest surrounding her, nor did she see Mother Nature in all her natural glory. She saw a wall, and it was closing in on her. She tried to stand, and as she did the blood drained from her head, and she passed out and hit her head.

In the same instant, Anwen saw Sekhet again, and she saw Teleri and her family and they were calling to her. She felt at peace and warm and safe and Anwen moved towards them and their love. Sekhet took her to the land of the great castles that reached up to the sky. She took her to the river where she had been once before. It was much changed. The fertile land had produced many crops and the fields were ripe for the harvest. There was an abundance of tall trees that produced a very sweet fruit. Sekhet was even more beautiful than she had remembered, but Anwen felt strange this time. Although Sekhet was aware of Anwen's presence it was as though she was not really there. Sekhet acknowledged her only when she was alone, and she noticed that none of the people who passed them by seemed to 'see' her. It was as though she was watching from afar. It was as though she had stepped into Sekhet's life.

She saw a man summon Sekhet. He told her that one of the pharaoh's brothers needed to see her. Sekhet cursed under her breath and indicated that she would make her way to see him. Being a young woman in her late adolescence made Sekhet very vulnerable. She was not only extremely beautiful, but as a virgin she was very desirable to the men of her time.

As a physician's daughter, though, she would not find it easy to get a husband since not many men wanted to marry a woman with so much learning. Her father spent many days trying to encourage her with her studies but tried to discourage her from being so forward with the knowledge.

Anwen looked around for Teleri and her family but they were nowhere to be seen. She realised that they would not be in this place. This was Sekhet's life, not theirs. Yet she somehow sensed that in this time she should look for them in the faces that passed her by.

Anwen hurried to keep close to Sekhet, for when there was distance between them she felt as though she was slipping back into the pain that had consumed her, and she was not ready to face that which she knew she had to face. Sekhet reached the bottom of the stairs that took you up to the doorway of the castle that reached into the sky. It was the biggest building she had ever seen. Each piece of stone was so closely laid to the next that you could not even push a leaf between the spaces. Anwen had no idea how these people could have constructed such a building and was even wondering if perhaps this was just another illusion created by her mind to help her ignore the pain of her own life.

She walked the stairs and counted 175 to the top. Two very tall men stood at the doorway. Their skin was a beautiful brown colour. Their bodies, naked to the waist, were oiled and glistened in the sun. Their hair was oiled and combed. It was smooth and sleek. They held spears twice their heights and were very overpowering. They both smiled as they saw Sekhet move towards them. They knew who she was. The pharaoh himself had passed an order for her to have access to this building and all within it. She wore around her neck the pharaoh's talisman. No one would dare cross her for fear of his wrath. Anwen realised that this was the same necklace that she wore and she tried to reach forward to take it from around Sekhet's neck. It was at this point that Sekhet looked her straight in the eye and shook her head. Anwen stepped back and tried to speak but found that her words were lost and all she could do was follow and keep close for fear of losing her way and finding herself back in the place she least wanted to be.

They moved indoors, and she was struck by how cool it was. The air was filled with the most wonderful scent. A scent that was as familiar to Anwen as the talisman around her neck. She realised that this was the same scent her mother and grandmother had brushed through her hair. She felt safe and happy.

Sekhet reached out and placed her arm around Anwen and drew her body close. Anwen closed her eyes, feeling the warmth of the embrace and how immediately she felt like there was nothing that could harm her. Sekhet kissed both her eyelids and her eyes felt cool and refreshed. Sekhet then turned and moved towards another set of stairs that led upward to a chamber where Anwen could hear shouting. Before they entered the room, she paused, and in what seemed longer than the minutes it took to convey this message, Sekhet explained to her how it was that she got to be in this place.

She told her the tale of that special day. The air was hot and dusty. Sekhet's mouth was dry and her feet ached. She was one of many walking through the desert. She could see her father and mother just ahead. The heat of the sand was distorting her vision. She could see the pharaoh and his entourage way ahead of the procession. Her uncle was a bearer and got to carry the pharaoh. He was tall and very strong. His olive skin was shiny from sweat, yet his face never showed any kind of distress.

Sekhet could not imagine how tired he must be, carrying the load of the pharaoh. She was so proud of him. She was so proud of all of her family. Her father held a very important place in the pharaoh's household, for he was the family physician. Her father was such a wise man and had taught her so much about the mixing of herbs—creating many cures for diseases that people would often die from. Sekhet spent as much time as she could with her father. She was so hungry for the knowledge. Anwen could picture her, only thirteen but very bright and very beautiful.

Her skin was a pale olive colour and her hair was long and black. She had the most incredibly large very black eyes . . . they were as dark as the dead of night and Anwen sensed that those that looked at her felt as though they were going to fall into infinity. She had long beautiful legs and when she walked she seemed to glide. She was mesmerising.

They had been on the road now for fourteen days and it would seem as though they would never get there. Her father had told her that just over the mountain range in the distance was a beautiful valley. It was green and lush and the most amazing river ran through it. It was a fertile land, and there they hoped to build a community and a life. Sekhet knew that because her father was so important they would be well looked after. The only thing she did not like was the way in which the pharaoh's brother looked at her. She had been helping her father tend to him. He had been bitten by a snake and because her mouth was small she had been given the task of sucking the poison from his leg. She told Anwen how he looked at her, even then, as she put her mouth over his wound. She raised her eyebrow and said to Anwen that she had wondered who the snake was and who was the most poisonous.

Even then Sekhet understood that she would have to make sure that she was never alone in the same room with him. This was not that easy since she spent many hours preparing the herbs for her father.

On one of the very long days that they moved towards this promised land, the procession had slowed down and there seemed to be some kind of great excitement up at the top. She told Anwen that she broke from the crowd and ran on ahead to see what all the noise was about. As she came to the front she saw that the pharaoh was very agitated by something. He was complaining that he had a toothache and it was giving him a terrible headache.

Sekhet could see her father way down in the crowd and knew that it would take him a little longer to get to the pharaoh, so she approached his entourage. Her uncle glared at her, indicating that she must not come forward; however, the pharaoh saw her out of the corner of his eye. He summoned her and asked her what it was that she wanted. He loved Sekhet, and as the daughter of his physician he had watched her grow into a beautiful young woman. He loved to tease her. As pharaoh no one dared question him or disobey him, but he had a soft spot for her and she knew it.

From beneath her robes she pulled out a pouch filled with a black powder. Sekhet got down on her knees and crawled forward to hand it to him. He reached down and pulled her to her feet and took the pouch from her hand. He asked her what it was. Sekhet told him that he should rub it into his tooth and the pain would go away for a while, at least until her father could mix up something for him to drink. He did as she instructed much to the dismay of his guards. Instantly the pain subsided. And that was how she got to have the talisman, for he rewarded her with it and placed it around her neck. Sekhet smiled remembering the joy she felt when her father finally caught up to her and was astounded to see his daughter with something so valuable.

Her uncle frowned and helped the pharaoh back into his resting place. They picked him up and continued onward.

As they entered the room, about fifteen people were standing around a very regal-looking man. Anwen could tell from Sekhet's body language that this was the man she had come to see but that she regarded him with disdain. As he saw her enter the room he shouted for the others to leave. They scurried off in great haste and left Sekhet standing alone. She bowed before him and passed a greeting of respect. The man stood up and moved towards the door way. He shouted out that he was not to be disturbed under any circumstance. He then moved towards Sekhet.

Anwen froze, for she could see the look in his eye. It was the same look she had seen in Cedrick's. Anwen tried to call out to Sekhet to run, tried to warn her of the impending danger. She tried to catch her attention but it seemed as though Sekhet could not see her. She was listening to what the man was asking of her. He was telling her that he had trouble sleeping—that he had not slept for almost ten days and it was making him irritable and anxious. He wanted her to massage his head in the way her father had taught her. Sekhet asked if she could call her father to come and help her prepare the oils that were required, and he very softly told her her father was not needed. He trusted her to be able to attend to his request. It was at this point that Anwen realised that Sekhet 'saw' her standing there and the two women shared an understanding of what was to pass. Anwen had endured the pain with Sekhet by her side and now it was to be Sekhet who would endure the pain with Anwen by her side. She very calmly moved about her duties. She prepared the oils that she would use to massage into this man's head, neck, and back. The pharaoh's brother was a big man. His body was overindulged and he looked as though he was heavily pregnant.

Anwen saw Sekhet cringe as she placed her hands on his body. She worked the oils into the muscles that were causing the restriction of the blood flow. As she moved towards his head the huge man reached out and pulled her down, throwing his weight on top of her.

Anwen ran forward and tried to pull him off Sekhet. He had his mouth over hers and Anwen could see the sheer terror in her eyes. She realised that she could not breathe and watched as Sekhet reached out and scratched at the man who was taking from her the only thing she had to give as an honourable woman. Anwen cried and tried to reach out to her. She felt again the pain of her assault but at that point remembered how Sekhet had taken her to the river and held her close till it was over. This was what she had known—for she had endured the very same thing all those years before.

In this time, at this moment, Anwen realised why it had been that she was able to accept her destiny so willingly. As they were struggling the talisman was torn from Sekhet's throat and Anwen reached out to pick it up. She held it in her hand (or it seemed as though she did) and stood and watched with horror as the man grew more and more frenzied. Anwen realised that he was euphoric with the power he had over this helpless creature beneath him. His desire for her consumed him. He was an evil, greedy man, and as Anwen looked into his eyes she realised that she was looking into the eyes of Cedrick. She realised that he had been in her life from the beginning of time—that it was her destiny to endure this again and again unless she found a way of freeing herself.

At that point of realisation the pharaoh's brother put his hands around Sekhet's neck and without realising his strength, in the fit of his ecstasy, he squeezed her throat, shutting the air to Sekhet's lungs. As she was struggling to breathe Sekhet looked at Anwen and calmness overcame her. A smile formed on her lips and she heard her say, 'I am Sekhet, and I will be reborn in you, and we will be avenged.'

Anwen turned and ran as Sekhet's soul moved out of her lifeless body. As Anwen moved out of the castle that reached to the sky she passed a man on his way in. She knew this to be Sekhet's father but in his eyes she recognised her brother Aneirin—there was a loud commotion and she could hear the pharaoh's brother calling out.

Sekhet's father stopped in his tracks, and she knew that he understood an awful truth. Just how awful she did not want to be around to witness. Sekhet was no longer there, and Anwen had to leave this place. Her purpose here had been realised and she ran and ran until she found that she was standing in front of the burnt remains of her family home. She ran straight into the arms of her mother. Her brothers and father came to be by her side and without speaking they walked through the forest to the spot beside the river where they had spent many a happy day.

They stood and embraced and Anwen could smell the ointment in her mother's hair and she again felt safe and at peace. Anwen could not endure the pain of the memory of Sekhet's attack, of how the poor girl had died. She realised then just how blessed she had been to have survived her encounter, that she had not died. That she had lived to share that night with the man she loved. She had lived to know the love of a man as wonderful as Winn. She realised then that she had moved a step closer to rectifying this terrible injustice. She reached for the talisman and realised that it was not around her neck, and she no longer had it in her hand. Again the panic rose within her.

Aneirin her brother took her hand and led her down to the river to the place by the bridge that he had built. There he showed her where the talisman was. It was wedged between the vines, caught like a spider's prey in a web. Anwen tried to reach out and free it but found she could not. After a time Anwen saw Aneirin moving off, so she gave up trying and followed him back to where the rest of her family were laughing and having fun. She forgot about the necklace and joined in, consumed in the happiness and love.

CHAPTER TWENTY-THREE

Here with her beloved family time had no meaning. There was no pain and no suffering. There was no loss, no commitment to be anyone except who you were born in this world to be. Anwen knew that there was someone missing in this family. There was a part of her that was missing but she could not think of that. To have that memory would take her away from her family and she did not want to go. She wanted to spend more time with them.

Anwen's father, Glendwyr, got up to go to the river and summoned them all to follow him. As they moved to the place where the tree stood Teleri came out from inside the tree. It was a joyous reunion, and although the family was now complete, Anwen still did not feel whole. There was a piece of her that existed but was not part of this world. She felt anxious when she thought about it. She knew that it was important for her to find that missing piece but she was not ready. Not yet.

They spent time together doing things that they had done as a family for many years. The longer they were together the stronger Anwen became. It was like the sun melting the ice from a young shoot. Anwen needed this time. She had endured so much on her own of late and apart from that one special moment she spent with Winn, there had not been any time for happiness and joy since her childhood. Anwen knew that something was missing and that she was needed, but she was not ready. Not now.

As she sat with her feet in the water of the river, she heard the song of her heart, the words resonating in her soul. She formed the words on her breath and hoped this would give them life. 'If I had known you but never loved you, my heart would only have sighed—but to have loved you and made love with you my heart gasped in rhythm with my soul and gave it wings to soar.' Winn—she remembered Winn and the forest and that special moment they had shared.

Anwen reached within her soul and finally understood what was missing. She had given birth to a child and knew why it was that she had to have this baby. The connection she felt reached through the ages. The baby that had grown within her belly was a child who would change the course of time. She was a human being who would have a far greater understanding of what the meaning of life was. This child would grow to be more than she had ever hoped to be. This child's heart was made of gold. This child knew that in order to change the course of time you had to put yourself first.

Anwen had a premonition of the daughter that she had birthed. A child that had been conceived in the direst form of conception would grow into the most ethereal angelic individual. The opposite of everything that was incomprehensible.

Anwen's child was regal and emanated an aura of understanding and love. As she grappled with the memory of the assault she saw Teleri in her mind's eye. She took that emotion of hate and disgust and stored it in a room in her heart where she knew one day she would have to open the door. One day she would have to walk into that room and learn to face the fact that there could have been no other way that her beautiful daughter could have come into this world.

Linn would be her name, and it meant 'waterfall' or 'lake.' She would be as fluid as a waterfall—her soul would boil over the ends of the earth and into the space of time and crash into a lake below where, in the still waters, all things that made life what it was would be nurtured and grow. From her position of power she would be able to steer the course of the river. She would be the river in which Anwen gained her knowledge. Her daughter would be the continuation of the source of comfort and understanding. Her daughter *was* the eternity of life and everything that Mother Nature embodied. Her daughter was born and her daughter's name had been written in the scrolls of time. Her daughter was Linn.

CHAPTER TWENTY-FOUR

Motherhood

The weeks that followed Teleri's death, were spent in a state of limbo. Anwen busied herself with the duties that were most expected of her, one of which being the most important task of all, motherhood.

Since spending time with her beloved family in a place that Anwen still could not find again, she came to understand that there was still much that she had to learn about. She was sure Teleri would have told her of such places, of such things, but sadly that was now not to be. She knew that she had 'the gift' and knew that she had 'the power', but it seemed that somehow it was just out of her reach. Anwen felt like she had just walked into a beautiful castle with many rooms, but for some reason she just could not open the doors to the rooms within the castle. Part of her was still missing. It was so frustrating, looking at where she needed to be yet not being able to get there.

Her little daughter seemed to flourish from day to day. It was the wonder of nature that even though Anwen had so much experience, she still felt like a novice.

There were so many wonders of holding a new life in your arms and watching it grow, watching it totally dependent on its caregiver. Anwen sometimes felt completely overwhelmed with the sheer importance of her love. She realised that everything she said or did from this moment on would impact the way in which her daughter would develop into a fully grown adult.

She remembered something her mother had once told her: that the most important part of being a parent was to always guide from a place of love. If you centred yourself in the midst of love, then everything that followed would come naturally and freely.

Her daughter never cried, never seemed discontent. She always smiled and spent her little days looking around at the world before her. Anwen watched, and it seemed to her that Linn was not in fact just a few weeks old but some years. It seemed to her that within the tiny frame she held in her arms there was an old and wise soul just longing to explore and express herself.

CHAPTER TWENTY-FIVE

Fane

After all the events of the past months—the looks of pity after Cedrick's sexual assault, the gossip that perhaps as a witch she would end the unwanted pregnancy, the jeers from those who thought she would now just become a harlot, and the death of Teleri—she felt 'different.'

After her moment with Winn, something had changed. He had unlocked a door within her that led to a place of discovery and desire. Anwen now understood the true meaning of being a woman. She was not only a 'spiritual' woman but was in tune with nature and with her body. Anwen had no doubt in her mind that she would need a husband. She would need someone who would love her for who she was. She would need someone who would accept her child and love her as his own. She needed a man to tend the fields, to hold her at night, and, above all, she needed a man to love.

The universe knew who this man was, and she had to be sure that she would open her heart to him since her heart already loved Winn and it would be more difficult.

Winn's constant assurances that he would make things right and that he would marry her always made her heart heavy. He was the eternal dreamer and was not 'gifted', and everything for him seemed a lot simpler than it actually was.

Anwen knew that she would not have him to herself in this life. She knew of the woman who would be his wife; she had seen it in the reflections of the river. She had not told Winn, for she knew that he was not yet ready to accept his destiny. It did not matter; it was not her story to tell.

She had no doubt, though, that the man who stepped into the void in her life would be as equally special and loved. Perhaps even more so since he would be the one who would have no other commitments, but would choose her over a less complicated relationship. Anwen realised that the universe was calling to her and that she needed to step up. She could feel something stirring within her, and it was a completely different desire. She remembered something her grandmother had told her. 'Truth', she said, 'is absolute, and truth, like love, is constant'. So she knew that the man who would come to her would be truthful and that his love would be constant and in its entirety he would allow her to explore the 'new' Anwen.

Two weeks came and went and even though each day she had made sure that she had been available to opportunity, it never came knocking. She was feeling particularly despondent and decided to pay Mary and Thomas a visit. She would take along a special pie, the one that Mary had been trying to get the recipe from her for years. She knew that Mary would always have some funny story to relate and it would help lift her mood, besides which she remembered that a family friend of Mary's was due to be passing through, and Anwen was quite intrigued since

Mary's eyes had had a definite twinkle as she was relating the story of her association with this particular person.

So she baked her pie and whilst it cooled Anwen decided she would take particular care on her appearance. She combed the ointment through her hair and then washed it off. It left such a beautiful scent and her already raven-coloured hair seemed even darker and richer and shimmered as she moved in the light. When it was almost dry she braided some flowers into the front of her hair, put on a clean dress, and as she turned to scoop up Linn from her cradle, she suddenly felt ashamed. She was far from perfect, and really, who would ever love her with everything that she brought to the relationship?

She sighed, picked up the pie, and made her way to Mary's. The day was clear and crisp, and as she made her way through her forest nothing else seemed to matter except that she was a woman with a perfect child walking through nature with hope and love in her heart.

She approached Mary's door, took a moment to straighten herself, and then knocked. She always loved to see Mary's welcoming face. Plump and merry, and when she smiled it reminded Anwen of a child who had just eaten *all* the pie. So as she heard someone approach the door, Anwen initiated the smile she was sure she would receive in return.

Anwen was so startled when the door opened that she nearly dropped the pie. For standing there was not the little round lady she had come to visit but a tall, incredibly handsome man. She stood for a moment still smiling, and as she looked into his eyes trying to gather her thoughts she noticed that he too was completely taken off guard by her appearance. She returned his gaze, and as steadily as she could she asked after Mary.

Anwen could hear Mary shouting for him to bring her inside. She handed the pie to him, and as his hand brushed hers she felt her knees grow weak. No one had had this effect on her before apart from Winn and no one told her that it would ever happen again. She didn't know it could happen again, and she nearly dropped Linn, who was looking up at the handsome man in equal fascination!

Once the introductions were done and the tea had been served and the pie cut, Anwen didn't really remember much of what was going on around her. She couldn't concentrate since each time he looked at her she felt like she was the only one in the room.

Fane was his name, and he was indeed the most intriguing person she had met in some time. His voice was deep but not harsh, and his gaze was intense but not lewd. She felt as though he could see the very core of her being. Winn was the only other man who looked at her like this, but because Fane was a commoner and had no commitments it opened up the world to a whole new set of rules. She knew that she stood a chance to be courted by this man. All manner of things were going through her head, and as he sat quietly watching her she felt as though he was reading her thoughts.

Fane briefly gazed at the little bundle that lay by her side squirming and softly gurgling, and his eyes softened as he asked her how many months old the child was.

Anwen felt oddly nauseous, for she sensed pity in his gaze. She felt faint and asked if she could step outside for a moment. The severe reaction this caused puzzled her and as she emptied the contents of her stomach under a tree, a soft breeze moved around her. The scent of the cipbar bush filled her senses. There was the familiar beautiful scent of an ancient intrigue. Her life was a puzzle of discerning and extraordinary moments. Anwen knew that this was a message from the ancient world she knew so well.

It was telling her that this was the man who would stand by her side, the man who would love her and keep her until her life was no more, and as she felt the blood drain from her head and her body sway she felt his arms around her. He caught her just before she hit the ground. His scent was strong and mixed with the scent of the cipbar bush; she felt as though she was in a trance.

She could hear him softly assuring her that she was safe. She could hear Mary shouting for Thomas to clear the bed and as he laid her down it took all of her will power not to draw him down on top of her.

What was she thinking? Who was this person who made her want to open the door to her desire? She lay there for a while to regain her composure.

CHAPTER TWENTY-SIX

Fane offered to accompany her back home, and as he picked up her basket in one hand and scooped Linn up in the other and pushed her through the door out into the world, Anwen knew that this was the moment; he was the one.

Her mind was racing and she felt oddly out of control. Normally so self assured and confident she found herself thinking that the journey home could go two ways. She could make idle chitchat, with long quiet pauses ending with a cordial thank you. Or it could be the chance for her to open her heart and her soul, bearing all to this man so that from the get-go he would know exactly who she was and what he would be getting himself into. Anwen knew which it would be!

He walked closely beside her, close enough but not touching her, occasionally glancing down at the precious bundle he was carrying. Linn was oddly quiet and Anwen kept checking to see that she was still breathing. She noted that her big green eyes were transfixed. Fane gently guided her over the terrain, pausing and pointing out when the ground was uneven, and every movement he took she felt was deliberate and conducted with genuine concern.

As they reached the stream and made their way across, over the bridge her brother had built, her grandmother had died on, she knew where it was that she would ask him to pause. They reached the other side and Anwen asked if he would go with her as she wished to show him something and wanted to speak with him. They made their way towards the tree, the ground thick with moss so she moved slowly so as not to slip. She gently moved the vines and leaves to expose the hollow within the base of the tree, and Fane was astounded and awed that she knew of such a place.

They moved inside where the walls of the tree glistened with sap. She seated herself in front of the place where she always made a small fire, and asked him to join her. He did not sit opposite her but directly next to her brushing the cold embers away from her skirts. He placed Linn in the crook of a root and made sure she was secure and warm.

Anwen watched his tenderness with her child and something compelled her reach out and take his hand and hold it to her face. Somewhere in her soul she knew this action would not be interpreted incorrectly, that this man understood her heart, and he did not pull away but with his other hand gently moved her hair from her face.

This action unlocked a door, and from it gushed her story, and not once did his gaze move from her face. She watched as his eyes softened when she told him of how it was she had come to become with child, how she had loved Winn, and how she had forsaken herself for the honour of the man she still loved.

He put his arm around her and drew her closer, and Anwen felt his breath on her face and his heart beating.

His chest was strong and warm and made her feel completely safe, and as she came to the end of her tale Fane continued holding her. She waited, afraid to speak or look up in case it ruined the moment, for to be held like this was something she had forgotten she needed, indeed craved.

After a while he took a breath to speak and what he had to say washed through her like a warm stream. It was as though she was speaking to herself. His words seemed to be a reflection of her thoughts and her hopes and dreams. Fane told her of his life. He told her of where he had come from. That he was one of two boys born to man who hunted for reward.

Fane went on to tell her that he had grown up in a loving family, that he had learnt the power and importance of love from his parents. His mother had been a hard woman but never failed to show her boys how much she loved them. Her actions always made up for her 'lack of sensitivity.' Fane's father was a very soft, gentle man with a huge heart, and he coddled and treasured his children. He took the time, Fane said, to always include them in his life. He hunted for a living and Fane's earliest memory was watching his father skin the animals he had killed. Fane explained that whilst his father was skinning the animal he would softly sing a tune that spoke of thanks, respect, and sacrifice. He remembered his father telling him that each animal taken by us for our needs should be treated in this way, for nothing in life should be taken for granted.

Fane had learnt how to hunt fairly and which animals to choose, and he never took more than was needed. Anwen smiled and quietly thanked Mother Nature for this man. He went on to tell her that growing up he had never met a woman he had been drawn to. He had never met a woman who he felt would be able to complete him, and he knew it was his destiny to wait. He shifted his body slightly away from hers and said that although he was a simple man the affairs of the heart were set in stone and when the right moment was presented we are all made aware of it.

His face coloured as he told her of how totally taken aback he had been when he opened the door and was presented with this fair-skinned, dark-haired beauty. He told her that at that moment for the first time in his life he had never wanted anyone so completely.

Anwen smiled and quietly thanked Mother Nature.

He then went on to tell her that Mary had told him a bit about her life and what and who she was to the community. He paused for some moments and said that he felt a little uncomfortable revealing his innermost thoughts since he'd been sure Anwen was betrothed to Winn, a lord, and he could not compete and would not interfere with Anwen's heart if her hand had already been offered. Anwen smiled and quietly thanked Mother Nature.

*

After their meeting, her friendship with Fane had grown and developed into something she never thought would happen. He made sure she was safe. He had helped her each day with the daily chores of living. He cut wood for her, helped her tend the fields, and carried water. She watched as he went about his tasks. Fane was such a beautiful man with such a wonderful soul. When he looked at her she knew that he wanted her, but his respect for her situation had always kept him from acting on it.

This was the day she had hoped that Fane would step out of what was expected of him and seize the moment to take what he wanted and needed. She was so sure that Fane was the man that she would be able to do this with, yet his caution to life was as strong as her gay abandonment of it.

He had for some months now been at Anwen's side almost daily. She wanted this man to be able to do something for himself, not because he knew that it was what Anwen needed. She was nervous and afraid, for the ravages of bearing a child had slightly altered her perfection and she felt as though he would be cheated. In their discussions over the time together Anwen had learnt that Fane too had kept himself pure. He had not been with a woman.

CHAPTER TWENTY-SEVEN

WINN

As Winn galloped off, he remembered how hard it had been to make his way with a heavy heart to see Anwen. Months had come and gone and life had seemed to settle to some kind of normalcy in the village. Fane was now caring for Anwen. The three of them had spent many moments of deep understanding and peace. He had hunted with Fane and watched as Anwen healed and grew into a woman he knew he could never have. The three of them became an unusual unit of love, but one that had no fruition.

His own situation in his household had changed. His father had been forced to accept an offer of marriage from a lord of a neighbouring Village. It would, after all, strengthen his position in the county. Winn knew that the war with the Mythrian army had taken its toll on the Raglands and in the Blathaon household. His father was getting older and more sickly, and as the only heir to the castle when his father had told him that the lady who had been betrothed to him, Morvudd, was on her way, and that her dowry had been paid, there was no turning back.

The demons in his heart tore at his soul. He knew that Fane would step in where he could not and his heart was filled with a mixture of jealousy and relief. In spite of himself he liked Fane, and had his affection been for any other woman, other than Anwen, he would not have even hesitated to give his blessing. Fane would care for this woman just as intensely as Winn would and he knew it.

He needed to hear it from her though. He needed to look into her eyes and see for himself that she was going to release him, he could not release her, and he never would, not in his heart that was. He envied her gift. He wished that he could see what she already knew. He asked for discernment but knew that his reaction would disappoint her. He was just a man, after all, and as he rode off he could hear Anwen shouting after him in pure frustration . . .

CHAPTER TWENTY-EIGHT

Anwen

Oh my God, can you even believe it! she thought. Anwen had given everything of herself. She had given her heart, her body, her soul. She had taken a risk and allowed herself to feel again. For so many years she had done all that was expected of her. She had followed all the rules and learnt all the lessons Teleri and Branwenn had taught her. She had spent so many years holding her feelings and emotions in check. Anwen had had a fire burning in the pit of her soul for so long, and just when she had accepted *who* she was the universe threw her a curve ball. She had done what she did best. She had taken broken and lost souls and nurtured them, loved and guided them back to life. Hers included!

She had stepped outside of the boundaries and taken a risk, and as she sat at the place she had so many times with Winn she thought her heart was going to break. She had just told Winn that she was considering Fane's proposal of marriage. He had not taken it well, and his obvious torment tore at her very being.

But she kept telling herself that she was bigger and better than that—she was Anwen born of Sekhet! She had endured. She had suffered the most a human being could have and had survived. So why then did it seem so hard? How was she going to 'fix' this?

It was an impossible situation.

She closed her eyes and quieted her soul and listened for the answer. And as she sat she heard the timeless voice of Mother Nature. Her words were like a soothing poultice on a very raw wound. A deep understanding washed over her. She had to understand that not everyone had walked the same path as she had. She was blessed and had lived so many lives. There would be people who would come and go who would leave her life having taken everything and leaving nothing. These were the people who would teach her the most. As she listened she made her way to the forest to the tree, to the life-giving river. She would make her way to the secret place where she and Winn had made love, to the place where the waterfall fell, to the source of the life-giving river—her river. She would make her way there and remove her clothes and knew that once she felt the water move over her body she would emerge refreshed and renewed.

Anwen had been reminded that people didn't define *who* we were. Life situations don't and can't change the direction of our lives. What we have to learn is to make sure that we are not affected, that we need to keep walking forward. Keep our eyes open and our hearts alive.

The love with which she felt for Winn and the desire to be loved and live a 'normal life' left her feeling so intensely sad that she was trapped in what could not be. She felt sad that since Winn did not have the enlightenment of centuries, he was not able to see the bigger joy. He had not yet learnt the joy of discovering *who* he actually was. He wanted everything. He did not realise that it was not within her capacity to deliver it, for she was not the ultimate creator of life.

As she reached the edge of the forest, Anwen stumbled and fell and rolled down a hill. Her elbow hit a rock and her hip grazed a tree stump. The physical pain mirrored the pain in her heart and she let out a cry of frustration and anguish, burning the back of her throat.

She had come to accept that her beauty was a curse, or it could so easily be so if she allowed it to be. She'd had had to sidestep the affections, attentions, and desires of so many men. She had kept herself pure. She had forgone her personal desires, just as her mother had instructed her. But Anwen was born to love. Anwen had been created for the purpose of love, and it was her destiny to love.

Love came in so many forms, and as she lay there she visualised the word. Winn had taught her to read and write, and the word 'love' filled her mind with so many visions. It meant so much to her. When she looked at the letter 'l' it reminded her of her tree—tall and strong. It was the pillar, the tower the strength for all those things that followed. The base of the letter 'l' was just like the roots of the tree, holding it strong and steadfast, nourishing and feeding it to help it keep growing stronger.

The letter 'o' reminded her of the sun and moon—two opposites of a life-giving force. Each had its own immense beauty and strengths and purpose—and life as all humans knew it to be could not sustain itself without either.

The 'v' was to Anwen the most beautiful. This reminded her of the one thing that all men desired, the 'sacred' place that men longed to be. This reminded her of the place where life was created and born. It reminded her of the place where immense joy and pleasure could be found. This was the place where the reward for hardship was given. This was the only place that could be found on earth where two humans could unite and transcend their souls to the sanctuary reserved only for the *gods*. The 'v' between a woman's legs was the place where heaven met earth.

The 'e' in the word love for Anwen was the perfect ending to a beautiful word—for when she looked at the 'e' she saw the spiral in the sea shell. It not only created an illusion of timelessness, it held a secret. It held its own unique and wonderful secret—for if you held the shell to your ear, you could hear the ocean. You could listen over and over to the gentle lap of the tide. It was the perfect end to a beautiful word, for love was an ageless and timeless spiral of beauty and joy and it was the one word which all humans coveted. It was the one thing that without which we would cease to exist. *Love* was the antithesis of *pain*.

So with this lesson, Anwen got up and brushed herself down. She made her way to the waterfall through the peace and quiet of the serene forest. The smell of the moss, the earth calming her soul and she exhaled all the pain of this lesson and she laughed and rejoiced in the many different areas of her life where *love* still existed. She was blessed. She was rewarded. She was woman, a woman with the power to create and renew, heal, and restore. Her destiny was to love and heal and her reward would be ageless and timeless. Anwen continued to make her way to the river, towards the waterfall, realising that life was not hard, it was a process of enlightenment.

CHAPTER TWENTY-NINE

As she made her way down to the waterfall, the feel of the moss beneath her feet, she heard the heartbeat of the forest she so loved. She had hoped that Winn would not disappoint her and mostly himself and that he would realise that this time would come and go and it could never be replaced. Each moment given to us is unique. She hoped that Winn would be able to realise just how much she loved him and wanted him to fulfil his purpose. Anwen knew the woman he was betrothed to was on her way. Winn could not deny it any longer. She knew that Winn liked Fane, for they had spent many weeks together in her company with Linn. The two men stood side by side loving her equally. All she wanted was to be able to live out her life as she had desired.

She wanted more so than any time in her life for someone else to take control and just take care of her needs. As she reflected, she let it go. It would be what it would be.

CAREW CASTLE, TENBY, WALES

The Castle continues to be in private ownership but is open to the public.

AUTHOR'S NOTE

As mystically as this story came to me, there were pieces of her life that were not revealed. I spent more than a year waiting for it to return. I visited the castle in Wales searching for the rest of the tale. How I came to discover that this was an actual place, and some of the events within this tale were documented history are a whole other story.

I considered filling in the spaces. So much of her life could have further made for an entertaining story. What did she feel when Winn married? Did she attend the ceremony? What did Winn feel watching her betrothed to Fane? Did they continue to spend time with each other? Did Winn's children get to know Linn? What was the great purpose of Linn's life to the history of Ragland? Why did she not have any other children? There are so many things still left untold. But just as mystically as it was made known to me, it has been mystically revealed that it was not for me to create these gaps. The purpose of this tale is far greater and that the parts of her life 'given' to me were a gift.

The resultant fact that my life has unequivocally changed direction has spurred me on to print the story as it was told in its mystical form. It is my duty only to document it. It has been life changing, and until the 'story', in whatever form it is, has been sent out into the world, I cannot rest. It is what it is and it is not meant to be anything more.

I hope that as my readers you will find enlightenment within some of the pages of this book. That the purpose of your life will be revealed and that you too will have the same depth of discernment that I have come to embrace in so much as, 'What has been written has been etched in time, for what was spoken and thought, has manifested physically'.

However . . . the tale did not end there. There was more, but only a little . . .

CHAPTER THIRTY

The consecration of Fane and Anwen

The water on her skin felt cool, and she could hear the beating of her heart as she floated on her back. As she lay there she recalled the words of her wedding vow to Fane. The words still fresh on her heart. **'I have consented to share a piece of my Soul with you. Our union is made with bonds of love and respect not ropes and chains. I do not own you and you do not own me but we have come together because the Universe conspired for us to meet. In our time together I want you to grow and be free. I want you to always follow your dreams. I want you to benefit from having known me, to enrich your life. I want to allow you to teach me things. I cannot promise that I will never disappoint you, but I can promise you, that to disappoint you, would be something I could not easily find in my nature to do'.** She had extended the invitation to him to join her at the river. She had indicated that this would be the day when his attentions would be rewarded.

She felt happy, their marriage had been a wondrous affair, and now it was time for her to finally give herself physically to a man for the first time. She was nervous but excited and had already made up her mind that she would not hold back. She felt the sun on her face, and as she let out a long sigh she felt movement in the water. Anwen did not open her eyes; she was aware that the beating of her heart was increasing and growing louder. Fane had undressed and had followed her into the water. The wedding party had dispersed, and they were alone at the pool at the base of the beautiful waterfall, the one that had so much mystical power and healing.

Anwen did not move, did not open her eyes. She knew it was Fane, and she smiled. Who else would it be? But what he would do in the next moment would define their future as a couple. He needed to take what he wanted. She could feel his movements by the stirring of the water and as he scooped her up out of the water his mouth was over hers. She opened her eyes and as she looked at him he told her of how much he desired her. How much he wanted to make love to her and how he could not live without her.

As he placed her on the banks of the river Anwen stepped into him and took his face in her hands and gently kissed his bottom lip, sucking it gently, tasting him, savouring the moment of all those practised thoughts. He responded just as gently and as she kissed him she could read his thoughts. She could see the events of her life past, of his life past, and she could feel that he was afraid and did not know how to proceed.

Fane asked her to please dry herself as he had wanted to take her somewhere special. He had averted his eyes, never once taking in her form beneath her wet wedding gown. It was incredible that even in his moment of need he had thought of her modesty. He walked away and let her dry herself in peace.

Anwen felt like the moment she had been waiting for had been suspended in time.

Fane helped her onto his horse and made his way back through the forest towards the sea. As they rode, Fane reminded her of the day she had expressed her desire to be by the ocean—to walk with the sand in her toes, to hear the crashing of the waves, to be one with the greatest rhythms of nature—the gentle and mysterious sigh of the life-giving ocean. The journey to the edge of the ocean seemed long, but she knew that once there she would be able to share so much life, so much of the wonderful world she knew so well—the place where the essence of our heartbeat existed, aside from 'her river.' She knew that the ocean was where our souls illuminated the earth with love.

She had put her trust in Mother Nature and the universe and she had been rewarded. As she held on to Fane everything seemed to fade, and she could see his beautiful hands, his smile. She felt his presence deep within her soul and recognised him from a time when they spent many hours laughing, living, and learning in another world. Anwen had known him before she had met him that day and now he had been delivered to her, and now they were here, in this moment, and it was her chance to just be.

There was a place he had found just off the beach, where a line of trees met the sand. There stood a tree that was so large, the inside of it could shelter two people from the weather and prying eyes. Her heart softened since she realised that he had tried to recreate 'her' special place, her 'beautiful tree', the place where they had sat and learnt of one another. As they slid off the horse without speaking a word, she took his hand and placed it on her breast over her heart, and he noted with surprise how fast it was beating.

As they walked towards the tree he knew what it was she needed from him—out of the sight of any other living human, he pulled her close and felt her naked body beneath the garments. Her scent was strong and intoxicating. It made him feel lightheaded. He slipped off her dress, and her nipples were hard but her skin was warm. Her breasts were soft and round.

He had never done this before and wanted it to be right. He knew she was his and she wanted to 'just be', so he laid her down gently and traced the shape of her body. He noted the colour of her nipples, the shape of her hip. She watched his hand as it moved over her body and arched her back and sighed; feeling him touch her drove her wild with desire. It was like a black hole that needed to be filled.

She wanted to give herself to him—to take him into that place that was reserved for her hunger. She drew him close and kissed his mouth. The smell of the wet leaves, the ocean, and his breath made her ache.

At that moment Anwen knew what she needed to do. She was no longer 'Anwen'; she was 'woman', and she took his hand and gently pushed his fingers deep into the wetness between her legs—it felt so good and she wanted so much more. Her pupils were dilated and her voice was deep and throaty as she turned to him and said, 'I want you to taste me, take me, love me, need me, feel me.'

Fane let himself go. Allowed himself to be taken in by this woman he had watched for so many months. As he gently kissed her body the memory of all that she had taught him, all that he had watched her endure completely consumed him. He moved his head between her legs and placed his mouth over her, wanting to know the essence of the woman he had come to love so deeply. He had never been with a woman before and knew that Anwen was no ordinary woman. He was afraid that she would be disappointed, but as he tasted her she gasped and writhed.

Her sweetness tasted like cooked potatoes.

Anwen thought she was going to explode, she couldn't wait. She wanted his hardness deep inside her, so she pulled him on top of her, and he slipped inside her, slicing into her silky wetness, thick and rich like warmed honey. She moaned and gasped, moving her hips to meet his rhythm. She didn't know this man as she was expected to nor did she care, all she knew was that she wanted him. That's all that mattered, that she was 'woman' and he was 'man' and they were in tune with nature and all that was meant to be.

Making love was what she knew she was born to do, and she knew that once he had shared this with her he would be complete. To be with Anwen like this was more than a physical experience; He knew it would rip his soul out and catapult it to another dimension. Who was this woman? Her long black hair matted with leaves and sand, her body wild with desire. He couldn't contain himself as he realised that *he* was the reason *she* was so wild. He wanted to feed her need—take her and give her the release she so longed for. She moved on him slowly, an urgency building deep within both of them, her breath on his face. She looked directly at him and pressed herself closer.

She moved faster, groaning and laughing, and he watched with fascination as her body suddenly froze, and he watched as she exploded in ripples of heat and release. Her body shuddered and writhed and her soul emptied itself and just as she came to the end of her wave she asked him to fill her. She wanted to feel him empty into her.

*

Anwen lay there so completely satiated and spent and she pulled the landscape around her like a blanket. Nature covered her with all that was pure. He had taken her back to where her soul had found its inception. Fane was so taken by the moment. She seemed to infuse him with life. To make love to this woman he had loved and watched was more than he had ever dreamed of. He knew that she had wanted him, and he had resisted until he had been given the right moment. He knew then that this was his destiny to love this woman for as long as he had breath in his lungs. He would care for her and protect her and her beautiful child as his own. *She* was his wife.

CHAPTER THIRTY-ONE

Linn's first lesson

Anwen watched her daughter laughing and running in the field that took them to the river. At eight years old she was a vision. Linn had the most beautiful head of auburn hair so dark it was almost the colour of congealed blood.

Cedrick's family all had had red hair and the combination of his and the jet black of her own made for a truly phenomenal creation. Linn looked like something that had been born of the mythical creatures of the forest. Linn had been a wonderful child right from the time she had entered the world. She had never cried. Anwen felt a pang of guilt when she remembered how she had awoken from her state of unconsciousness after some time had passed to realise that the baby she had just given birth to was lying quietly looking up at her mother, waiting patiently for her to come back.

Anwen knew that it was not normal for a newborn baby to be so quiet and still. How grateful she was that the forest had kept her safe during that time when the ravages of all things cruel could have taken her. At a time when Anwen wasn't sure she could even love this child. She remembered how when she had woken and looked down on Linn, how her daughter's perfect little mouth seemed to be set in a smile. It's how she remained, and that smile grew into laughter.

Linn was a small elfin child in stature but her nature was as big as the tree that grew by the side of the river. Her skin was pale and her eyes were green. She looked, Anwen smiled, much like a wood fairy. She remembered gently stroking her daughter's little face and telling her that as she entered this world she would need to live her life with perfect love and perfect trust—harm no one ever, for this was the key to her success.

From that moment on Linn loved to be outdoors. She loved to be close to nature and was not afraid of anything strange or new.

Fane had gone hunting. Winn had asked if he could please stock the kitchens of Ragland Castle for the celebratory feast of the anniversary of his marriage to Morvudd.

On this day Anwen had decided that she would take Linn to the river and show her the whereabouts of the secret hollow within the tree. She knew that at eight years old Linn would fully understand the significance of its majesty and the importance of keeping its location a secret. Linn was heaven's gift to Anwen.

There was so much in life for her to be and so much for her to see—she had a great responsibility to put her on her pathway to her destiny.

There was a storm on the horizon and she wanted to take her up the side of the mountain to collect the leaves of the cipbar bush to make the ointment for their hair, and she had decided that she would send this along as a gift for Morvudd. Anwen remembered Teleri and felt her strong in her heart. She missed her grandmother and had so wished that she had lived to see Linn grow and to meet Fane. She sighed, yet in spite of her thoughts she felt on fire on this beautiful day; the air was thick with promise.

She felt intensely aware that something of great significance was going to happen. She was afraid and excited. In the winds of the storm Anwen heard her grandmother's voice whispering. Anwen's heart skipped a beat, the sound of her grandmothers voice was like rain falling on the water. She strained to hear her say, 'When the dark tree fell before me, I closed my eyes and saw the ocean, my ocean of my childhood and I was not afraid, so I opened my soul to the sea. As I lay there at the mercy of that storm, when that dark night seemed endless, I asked the forest to please have you remember me. The river enveloped me, and I want you to know that though we shared this humble path, as I lay there alone I realised how fragile my heart was.

'I called to Mother Nature to give my feet wings to fly, to reach up and touch the face of the stars, and that is where you will find me from this moment on, in the heavens watching over you and Linn. Guide her with love, Anwen, and protect her, for she will on this day open a door to forever change the history of Raglands. I see you and the man you are with and I am pleased.'

Anwen felt the caress of Teleri's hand across her cheek and became aware that Linn had stopped doing what she was doing and was watching her. She said, 'I hear her, Mummy.' It was as though she too could hear her grandmother's voice and felt the light of her soul pass through both of them and at that moment the tears of happiness welled up. Could life have been any more beautiful? What had she done to deserve this wonderful gift? What had she done right to be in complete unity with creation and to feel the heartbeat of the world coursing through her veins?

CHAPTER THIRTY-TWO

Reflections of Anwen

Anwen made her way up the side of the mountain. She was tired, and her body was not as young as it used to be, but she knew that she needed to make this journey one last time. As she moved up the air grew thinner, and it was more difficult to breathe. She wished she had brought herself another skin of water; one was not going to be sufficient. Her resolve grew stronger, however, as she passed the mental milestones of her life, and when she finally reached the top she sat down on the edge of the precipice whilst she gathered her strength.

She had forgotten how far it was since the last time she had made this journey, and Winn had carried her some of the way. Her heart filled with a renewed strength and she stood up and walked across the top of the mountain. Its circumference was small, yet big enough to feel safe. She felt like she was the 'queen of the castle.' She walked across the top and looked out across the valley. Spread beneath her was her beloved forest.

Through the trees she could just see the place where her father had built their family home, a place that was now just a memory of ashes. She could map out the journey she took through the forest. She saw the place, the sacred place that she had shown Winn and her heart filled with love as she remembered that night she had spent in his arms. She saw the place where 'her' tree stood, across the river that was so much more than just running water. It was the place where life as she knew it had sprung forth. Over to the other side was where the castle stood. Its walls stood strong. The history of its occupants stored for all time within, beating with the sound of the heartbeats past and present.

How changed the castle was from the first time she had laid eyes on it, that day her father had taken her to see it. Anwen stood watching the sun move down to meet the night and she closed her eyes. A breeze washed over her and caught her, tossing her long now-silver hair to and fro. She knew that she had to be here to take the time to regain her strength for perhaps one last important task in her life.

As she took the air into her lungs she felt the presence of Teleri, of her mother, father, and brothers, and of loved ones past. She saw the light of her soul scattered through her lifetime, gently resting on the shoulders of those who had walked through the doors of her life—a light that left her essence, her love, her hopes, and her dreams. And as she turned her back on what was, she looked to the future—an old woman, not a girl. So many memories, so many lessons. She hoped that the light of her soul would continue to touch people's lives and help them realise their dreams as she soared to continue to reach hers. She still had so much to do with her life, but as she stood there on the verge of something great she realised that unless she had the resolve, unless she asked for help, she would not fulfil her destiny.

Anwen had come to understand the meaning of life. She felt no remorse, no regret. She had been given the knowledge and understanding that everything that had passed through the doors of her life was planned. She understood that in order to be the person she was today she had to endure the life she had lived.

CHAPTER THIRTY-THREE

The end of it all

As Anwen lay there, her heartbeat slowing, her life passed before her mind's eye. She saw the castle, and in the face of her beautiful daughter, Linn, she realised she had never been happier. Raglands had been the place where she had been free. Free to be a whole human being. Free to express herself without judgment. She had been loved and revered and knew that the imprint of her soul was in this place and would be there for all time.

One day she would return, and at that moment she understood. She realised the purpose of her life. She had a deep understanding of her worth in this world. She understood that all of her actions in this life had affected someone and that, in fact, as a result of her, their lives had forever been changed. She understood that she would leave this time having achieved a great lesson. Her life had been happy and free.

She caught a glimpse of Sekhet. She saw how she had not been free and had not had the opportunity to learn the lesson of her life. Sekhet had learnt her lesson through Anwen's life.

She caught a glimpse of a time to come when she would one day remember this life at Raglands; she knew with joy in her heart that she would return again to this wonderful place and would again be reminded of the lesson learnt in this life.

She reminded herself again of what the lesson was. That we are all unique and important individuals, that we are all on a journey, that we have the right to be free to be who we are supposed to be in order to fulfil our purpose in the world. That we are free to choose who walks this journey of our time on this Earth with us, and to love and be loved is the greatest gift of all.

As Anwen lay there, her heartbeat slowing, she saw her daughter at her side, she saw her granddaughter, and she saw her beloved Winn and her beloved Fane. She felt whole and warm and content, and as she took her last breath she smiled at them all and said, 'Thank you'.

At the time of Anwen's passing her body seemed to emanate a light. The air was filled with the fragrance of honey and earth and cooked potatoes. The trees stirred and the leaves sighed. Later, when she was buried in her beloved untamed forest, the tree that grew at the head of her grave grew tall and strong. No one knew what tree it was, but it produced a beautiful white flower that bloomed all year round. The berry within the flower would be harvested and crushed for its oil, the fragrance of which smelt of honey, earth, and cooked potatoes and had a healing property that no one could explain.

CHAPTER THIRTY-FOUR

Winn stood on the bank of the river by Ragland Castle. He moved to the bench he had sat on with Anwen that day she had told him of the whereabouts of Bronwen's body. He looked towards the untamed forest, and he felt as though his heart would break. He could not comprehend the fact that his Anwen had died.

He heard his wife and children within the castle grounds and remembered who he was. He was Winn, lord of Ragland Castle. He had loved a woman whose life had healed and touched so many others, including his own. He had been loved by her and remembered the precious times he had shared with her, holding her, breathing in her scent. He remembered her laughter and her joy of life. He knew that one day he would find her, as she had explained to him the promise that they would have the chance to live a life as one soul. He closed his eyes and took a deep breath and was sure that he could smell her, that familiar smell of honey and earth and cooked potatoes, and for a moment he swore that he heard her whisper into his ear: 'Take me with you in your heart and feel me holding your hand through this life and into the next . . .'